4/03

THE BRASS BED

and other stories

THE BRASS BED

and other stories

by Pearl Cleage

Third World Press • Chicago

First Edition 1991
First Printing 1991

ISBN: 0-88378-127-1
Library of Congress Catalog Card #: 90-070705

Cover illustration by Patrick Hill
Cover design by Gina Minor

Manufactured in the United States of America

DEDICATION

For my daughter, Deignan Cleage Lomax; for my life's companion,
Zaron W. Burnett, Jr.; for my friend to the grave, Walter R. Huntley, Jr.;
and for my fellow traveller, William D. Bagwell.
For their unconditional love.

For my sister, Kristin Cleage Williams, the mother superior; my father,
Jaramogi Abebe Agyman, the master teacher; my stepfather, Henry W.
Cleage, the sage of Watermill Lake; and my mother, Doris Graham
Cleage, the first storyteller, for raising me right.

For my friends Mongo Lee, Carolyn Monteilh, Melanie Lomax,
Cecelia Corbin Hunter, Ingrid Saunders Jones, Johnetta B. Cole, Susan
Taylor, Woodie King, Jr., and Michael Lesy, with love.

And for my wild family, with affection and respect.

Table of Contents

Can You See Them?

I been ridin through America
like an orphan child
with no momma's lap
no Christmas tree,
no daddy's arms
to hide in, glide in, slide in
and wait out the storm.

I been ridin through America
stomach full of rum-spiked coffee
and ice cold beer. Stomach full
of Eggs McMuffin and Quarter Pounders
with cheese.

I been ridin through America,
lookin at Tennessee,
listening to Kentucky,
crossin the Ohio River on the run,
even though I don't have to anymore,
no matter what they say,
or how loud they say it.

I been ridin through America,
ears on fire like nobody's child,
and everybody's b/a/b/y,
singin that country song
where the woman says:
Cuz I still love you,
or at least I think I do.

3

And we laugh at how free we feel,
out together, ridin through America,
and then we round the curve
of that mountain road
and we gasp and holler
at the beauty of the land,
and it makes us love each other more.
It makes us love our children
and our mothers and our fathers,
and our grandmothers,
and our grandfathers,
more and more and more and more...

Sometimes we think we see our ancestors
walking up these rivers
in the mist. Sometimes we try
not to talk about it.
But then he will say:
Can you see them?
Dropping his voice like spirits
can't hear all the way down
into your very soul
even if you whisper.

Can you see them?

And I want to tell him:
No, I don't see anything.
Can't you see I'm busy
ridin through America?
But: Yes, I say. Oh, yes,
I see them. I always see them.

Sometimes their presence makes us

want to pledge something.
We want to promise to always
do thus and so, forever and forever,
to the absolute grave and beyond
where there is only energy and light
and wind and then the stillness.

Sometimes their presence makes us
weep and cuss and wonder
how and when and where and why
they died here. And how come
when they told Beulah Mae Donald
that the Klan had lynched her son
in downtown Mobile, Alabama on March 21, 1981,
she closed her eyes and thanked her god

because at least they hadn't thrown
his mutilated body into the river.
And what kind of something is that
to be thankful for?

Nobody wants to think about race
all the damn time.
Even me. Especially me.
I'd rather think about love,
and how to get hold of that picture
my sister has of my mother,
looking like a bohemian intellectual,
glasses perched on the bridge of her nose,
cigarette dangling from her longer-
than-I-remember-them fingers.
I'd rather think about my fat little nephew
blinking up into his first snow,
and my Uncle Louis' poem
about the high bouncing lover

in the bright gold hat.

I said nobody wants to think about race
all the damn time.

I hadn't seen that face for a week,
but I recognized it instantly.
The way his skin stretches over the bones

like it's about to tear. The eyes.
We've only been back in the city one day
and he is already pacing.

No, I say, teasing, trying
to make him smile, hugging him tighter than I meant
            to:
You can't go and you can't move.
That's what they all say, he says,
and moves my arms from around his neck
and moves my arms from around his neck.
Openness to me is openness to them,
and we all know the penalty for that.

Better to close the house, pack a bag,
check the tires and hit the road.
It's harder to hit a moving target anyway,
which is why I been ridin through America,
runnin through America,
trying to pretend it's Christmas,
and hoping this time
the river won't be so cold
and we can make it all the way to Canada.

The Brass Bed

The lineage runs through the women. Because of the children. And the bed. Or maybe that's saying the same thing twice. Or once removed. No matter. It was a lot of different things for the men. Mostly land. Sometimes gambling. But for the women, it was always because of the children that they made a move or didn't. Left a man, or stayed. Their choices were more limited.

The problem is in getting ahead of the story, or refusing to get behind it, or thinking there is no story. Begin at the beginning.

It was 1885, give or take a year on either side. There were thirteen sisters and their mother had been born a slave. Abbie and Jennie were the oldest and the youngest, respectively, and they lived outside of Montgomery, Alabama. Their mother was a seamstress and they spent their days bent over bolts of New York silk, translating the latest Paris styles into an acceptable Alabama facsimile for the genteel white ladies who oohed and aahed over the fineness of their stitches and bemoaned the rising cost of southern chic.

It was hard work and their mother demanded silence to insure concentration. After a few years of this, Abbie, in a fit of passion and defiance, married herself off to a riverboat gambler with a dimple in his chin and a cruel mouth who beat her, threw her children into the street and locked the door behind them. He travelled the Mississippi bringing home not money for food and children's clothing, but trunks of satin dresses, thick golden rings, diamond studs and bottles of expensive cognac.

In a poker game on one such trip, he badly beat a hard-eyed man without a sense of humor, who waited until he slept and then slit his throat from ear to ear. Frightened and alone, Abbie became the mistress of the town sheriff who bought her a small house on the outskirts of town so that he could visit her in safety, away from the eyes of his white family. She felt safe there, until the sheriff was killed by a man who made his living selling moonshine whiskey.

Desperate and weary, Abbie went to live with her sister who, by this time, had married a musician, presented him with two daughters and watched him die of stab wounds at a church bar-b-que that got out of hand. It was too much. Abbie and Jennie, clutching their few belongings and their children, fled Alabama in the midst of a summer Yellow Fever quarantine and settled, breathless and amazed, in Detroit, Michigan.

Jennie soon returned to Alabama, frightened more of the North and its grime than the South and its fevers. She married one last time to a small, very jealous Italian who hid himself on the street, watching her pass, undetected, making sure she walked alone. He fathered her last child, Alice, who contracted polio as an infant and carried a small, twisted leg as a reminder for the rest of her life.

Jennie's oldest daughter, Fannie, was a bright girl who helped out in the grocery store owned by an uncle, once removed. She was well known in the neighborhood for her ability to add long columns of numbers in her head, rapidly and without error. She remembered many years later the off-color remarks of the white men who came to the store to tease and transact business with the slender, green-eyed black girl. "I would just press my lips together," she remembered, "and look North."

Looking North with the same determination was Mershell C. Graham, a hard-working, sober man who was looking for a good woman to share his life and bear his children. Fannie promised to wait for him, and he went North, to Detroit, at

8

Abbie's urging, found the job at Ford that he would keep for the next forty years, and saved his money so he could send for his fiancée.

One day in the midst of his waiting, he passed by two policemen setting furniture out on the street from a recently raided house of ill repute. They set a bed down in front of Mershell, swore softly at each other and went back inside. He had not been in the market for a bed, but this one, *this* one, was made of thick, highly polished brass and when Mershell saw it, magnificently blocking his path home, he reached into his pocket, peeled off five one-dollar bills and rescued the bed from an unknown fate. He soon sent for Fannie and went about settling down to raise a family, being careful, of course, never to tell his wife that the fine brass bed in which all four of her children were conceived had first been home to the more practiced moves of big city prostitutes and their johns.

Shell and Fannie had four children: two sons and two daughters. One son died at the age of three of Scarlet Fever and the other was run over by a truck a few blocks from home and died in the street calling for his mother.

Mershell and his youngest daughter were once hit by a train which he could not see coming because of one blind eye, the result of a hunting accident. His daughter, who saw the train coming, was too embarrassed to mention it to him for fear his feelings might be hurt because he could not see it for himself and remove her from danger. No matter. They were not hurt and walked home, exhilarated by the adventure and assuring Fannie that yes, they were still very much alive. Yes, yes. They were very much alive.

Jennie missed her sister and her daughter and soon moved to Detroit with her two remaining daughters, Daisy Pearl and Alice. They found work as seamstresses in a fine fur store downtown sewing purple silk linings in midnight-sable coats.

9

In poor health now, Jennie kept their house for them and spent the last years of her life fussing and giving orders from a wheelchair. When Jennie died, she left a space in the lives of her daughters that they filled with her memory and regular Wednesday night cards with a few female friends.

One evening, Alice and Daisy had dinner, played a gentle game of dominos, drank a small glass of sweet red wine between them, and retired to the double bed they had shared since they were children. In the morning, Alice found Daisy sleeping more heavily than usual, but did not wake her. Two days later, she called Fannie, asking in a whisper for her advice on the matter. When the funeral home came for the body, the small house was sickly sweet with Alice's efforts to disguise the truth with a dark blue bottle of *Evening in Paris* cologne.

Alice moved in with Fannie after that, but she was never the same. She had come to occupy that position she dreaded most: the spinster sister come to live alone in an upstairs room, memories taped to the edges of her mirror. But she spared herself that loneliness. She fled from that upstairs room by refusing to believe that she was there at all. Family dinners became tense with Alice giggling at someone no one else could see. Alice, muffling laughter in her hand, whispering: "Please don't make me laugh! You know they can't hear you!"

After a while, they put her in an institution and visited her every other Sunday, until Fannie died and then it didn't seem to matter much. Her absence passed through the family with barely noticeable murmurs.

Jennie Turner is my great-grandmother. Abbie Allen my great-great-aunt. Mershell and Fannie Graham my maternal grandparents. All gone now. Except what they remembered and told. And except the brass bed from the house of ill repute. It now belongs to me.

Lessons

My mother put tap dancing in the same category as cheerleading and pierced ears. It was something you did only if you didn't know any better. It was something some black people did, but that *we* did not do because we were aware of things they didn't know yet.

Not yet, my mother would say. She was tired of having this "can't we puh-leez take tap instead?" discussion every time she dropped my sister and me off for ballet at Toni's School of Dance Arts. We knew she was tired before we asked the question, but we had to ask it every time. We didn't want her to change her mind without telling us. We didn't want her to turn to us, years later when we tried to prove that she was responsible for our current, sorry adult state, and say: "I changed my mind about that whole thing. I even remember when. It was that week it rained so much. But you never asked me again. Why should I have been the one to bring it up? I thought if it was really important to you, you'd mention it. But you didn't, did you?"

We didn't want her to smile that smile, proving to us once again that she had been more than just a *good* mother. She had been a smart one.

So we asked, and she denied, and our lust intensified and turned in on itself until tap dancing took on the importance of sacred rite in our lives. We would stand in the hallway and watch the tap dancing class go through their latest routine with a reverence that I have felt for few things since. (Bob Marley being a notable exception.)

"Tap, tap, slap! Tap, tap, slap!" Toni would be screaming from the front of the room, her back to the class, her eyes riveted to their reflected feet in the mirrors. "Tap, tap, slap!" And she would wave her long arms, clapping in time with the rhythm of all those shiney black shoes. "Smile," she would say, insistent and breathless as a lover. "Smile," as if secrets would be revealed, boulders would roll from tombs, lives would be saved and orgasms eternally achieved if they could only learn to *smile*.

Those who had momentarily forgotten would hear her voice through their brow-furrowed concentration and drag up the corners of their mouths, skin their lips back over square, white middle-class teeth and just smile awhile.

A few minutes later in ballet class, Toni acted like she didn't even know the word for the phenomenon known as smiling. She left her volume in the tap class and brought with her only a hiss: "Straighten that back!" or "Watch that turn-out!" Never "Smile!"

She probably knew it would have been useless in ballet class anyway. Those of us in ballet had parents who were concerned about culture and propriety and keeping our dresses below our knees. They had spent many hours teaching us not to smile at strangers and white folks. Our rapid generalization of this command accounted for the sullenness which was our usual expression. Smiling was not a priority.

But the tappers' parents knew where the goat was tied. They were raising children who could keep a smile in place during the most intricate maneuvers. The more advanced among them had even learned to complete complex multi-rhythmic steps without once licking their lips.

I used to wonder if any of the girls in the tap class would care if they found out what my mother was saying about their invisibility. My mother claimed they were all invisible and would probably remain so. "Their parents have never read Ralph Ellison," she would say. "Doomed to repeat history time after time, straightened head marching after straightened head, because they will not read Ellison."

We were older, of course, before we realized that Ralph Ellison was regarded by most people who took notice of him at all as a fine writer about whom it was often said: "too bad he never wrote another novel," but by only a very minute group as the most neglected prophet of his time and potential savior of The Race. My mother fell into, perhaps totally comprised, the latter group. After she said that his book, *The Invisible Man*, had taught her everything she knew, I scanned its pages for weeks looking for some prohibition against tap dancing and pierced ears before realizing that once she had gotten the basics down, my mother was prepared to improvise on the details.

But she was convinced of the tappers' invisibility just as she was convinced that pierced ears lead to dope smoking and indiscriminate kissing after school. My sister and I had no evidence to refute her. We did have strong evidence that, invisible or not, the tappers had style, a style I was convinced would sustain them even in the face of their own invisibility.

I wondered if they would be frightened or concerned. They didn't look to me like they would ever be frightened or concerned about anything. I can assume now that my impression had more to do with gross misinterpretation on my part than with any kind of collective optimism on theirs, but admittedly, this is hindsight. At the time, I was convinced that they smiled because the joy of "tap, tap, slap," was far greater than that to be found in an equal number of *pliés* or *grans jetés*. I believed that their sheer smiling pleasure in doing what they were busy doing in that hot little room was proof that this kind of dancing was worth the risk. Invisibility seemed a small price to pay.

My father took this desire for tap shoes as evidence of weakness in my genetic make-up, inherited, of course, from the nameless white ghosts skulking in our blue-veined past. Maybe he was right, or that may have been his way of trying not to blame himself. My father is, after all, maybe even above all, A Race Man.

My mother blamed it on the forces of invisibility and refused to look any closer than that. My mother was also the first person to make the distinction for me between truth and foolishness, and she, certainly, was no fool.

The Letter

The winter that she graduated from college, my older sister, an artist, packed her paints and sketchbooks in a knapsack, double-looped a soft blue scarf around her neck, stuffed her hands into the pockets of her peacoat, suffered through one more tremulous, teary hug from my bewildered mother, grinned at me, gaping at her from inside the safe circle of my father's arm and climbed on a bus headed for San Francisco.

In addition to her paints, my sister carried clean socks, a pair of Mexican silver earrings that swung against her neck when she walked or turned her head, one hundred dollars in five-dollar bills, and a small notebook whose untouched pages were to tenderly record the revelations she had no doubt would unfold along the endless stretches of highway between Detroit and the shimmering, magical, ocean-bounded west coast.

She also carried a letter which I had worked over, revised, edited, typed and retyped with great concern and presented to her that final night before her leaving. I was filled with sadness that she was going so far away and awestruck that she had actually purchased a bus ticket, made clear to family and friends the absolute necessity and irrevocability of her decision, and was now serenely going through her books, rereading favorite passages so they would be clear in her mind for recall during the lonely silent bus hours when those more jaded than she would be sleeping while my sister's eyes remained open, trying to watch everything, even in the dark.

But the letter. She carried the letter on the bus with her, assured me she had read it several times already and planned to do so several times more. She knew I had labored over it because I loved her and was disgusted with my own cowardice which

15

was all that kept me from going with her. So she took the letter as proof of sisterly devotion and never questioned me on its bizarre, depressing contents, which included a general admonition to be very careful and write home frequently and then several pages of neatly numbered rules and guidelines for clean living that I was afraid she might forget in the dazzle and sweetness of living her own life on her own terms. These included everything from a reminder not to speak to strangers of either gender to an incredibly naive warning against consuming any of the wide variety of illegal drugs I imagined were being forcibly thrust upon innocent young artists from the Midwest by vast hoards of sinister west coast dope dealers.

Years later, in a conversation conducted in whispers and giggles so we would not awaken her small children sleeping in the next room, my sister revealed to me that as the bus barreled along towards San Francisco, the fears and guilts crawling all over my letter started to get to her. She felt them pulling against her flight, grounding her in a past she no longer chose to claim. So she muttered an apology to me, blissfully unaware back in Detroit, tore the letter into unreadable shreds and tossed it out somewhere just before the bus crossed the border into California.

I was hurt to hear it, even after all these years and decisions later, but I knew she was right. I have never been an adventurer. I am too careful, too aware of the dangers. I spent too many years listening to stories of lost little girls who, despite warnings, rode their bikes one more time around the block after the sunset and were never seen again. Strolling along up and down strange streets at odd and sunless hours serves only to frighten and depress me.

But in spite of my own cowardice, or maybe because of it, I am an unabashed admirer of wanderers. Greeting a long lost friend as he falls exhausted into my house at 5 a.m. after a wild,

16

exhilaratingly dangerous trip through the Middle East, I search his tired eyes for secrets. Reading Jack Kerouac, I begin to scribble in my journal of unanswered longings for "the road," and confess in a letter to my sister that I am hungry to take a bus trip across the continent. Her answering letter first brings me up to date on the growth of her four young daughters and then warns against the journey after which I am lusting.

"Don't do it," she writes to me. "The bus is horrible and crowded and takes forever. The food you get is awful and everybody in California is crazy or high. Somebody I didn't even know tried to kiss me on the street in Berkeley, and that was 1968!"

She didn't warn me not to speak to strangers, but almost. I saved her letter though, folded carefully in its envelope of recycled paper. I know she wrote it because she loves me and is disgusted at the mutual cowardice that we each wear now with the ambivalent pride of a woman in her first maternity clothes. I know that when I tear it up just outside of Salt Lake City, she'll understand.

Reconciliation

My sister and I
have found each other
after all these years.
Found a place
that allows us to remember
those whisper sister years
of sleeping in the same room
holding hands in the monster filled dark
between our narrow beds.

I listen to her voice
as we laugh together
across the miles
around the years
and I tell her it was cheaper
when we settled for a letter or two
and maybe a box at Christmas.
So what, she says.
It's only money.
I'd rather have
you.

A Paris Of The Mind

When I first met Lucius, I had just turned 20 and he was barely 13. I had complicated both of our lives by first marrying his older brother and then appearing at his front door for the required once-over which is the bane of every new bride's existence. Since such introductions usually proceed along the household's normal chain of command, by the time I got to Lucius I had already been through an acid-tongued mother, a trio of intensely eccentric older sisters and a next-to-the-last kid brother who was quietly plotting to graduate from high school and run away to Harvard.

Although my new husband shared the concern of his family over his baby brother's recent behavior, which ranged from skipping school to stealing a dime store packet of brightly colored plastic combs, I liked him almost immediately. He was perceptive and irreverent and funny and we laughed at enough of the same bad jokes that, given half a chance and a more neutral environment, I had a feeling we'd be friends.

And I was right, although I had to wait 10 years for the proof. By that time, I had settled into my life in Atlanta and Lucius had graduated from high school, dropped out of college and left the country to seek his fortune and write a book. In the time honored tradition of expatriate American writers from Ernest Hemingway to Richard Wright, he went first to Paris, then to Israel and finally to Greece where his carelessness or simple naivete landed him in jail for smoking hashish. A clerical error put him back on the street the next day and, with a presence of mind that still amazes me, he went immediately to the American Embassy, called my husband for emergency funds and bought a plane ticket to Atlanta.

19

He arrived at five a.m., exhausted, exhilarated and carrying a draft of his first novel. Perhaps in gratitude for my willingness to allow him to camp out at our house or in recognition of my own aspirations as a writer, he handed the manuscript to me before collapsing into a deep, twenty-four-hour sleep.

His book was wonderful. Hip and wise and real and sexy. His beautifully straightforward prose described a life so far removed from my own it was as if he had dropped in from Venus. I was impressed and a little envious and my laughing confession of both emotions and his shy delight in my response mark in my mind the moment we gave up being in-laws and decided to be friends.

It has been a challenging relationship and a delicate one. Lucius was a house guest during a period of my life that was difficult at best, but our relationship was sustained by a shared love of words, a determination to Get To The Bottom Of Things and an ability to inhabit a Paris of the mind. In Lucius' case, it was, in truth, more than a fantasy. He had been there, bumming around, drinking Pernod in sidewalk cafes, writing. His adventurous tales of bohemian life reassured me that the world did not begin and end in my manicured backyard and gave me hope that one day I would be strong enough to become the writer I wanted to be and make a pilgrimage to Paris. I clung shamelessly to his descriptions, his memories, his plans to return and he spun his tales like a slightly more rumpled and decidedly male version of Scheherazade.

It was during one of these discussions that the idea of buying me a ticket to Paris first occurred to him. He said, knowing me, I'd be too chicken or too practical to spend my own money to do it, no matter how badly I wanted to go, so he thought he'd facilitate the process. The idea had a certain appeal, although at the time Lucius was as broke as I was adrift and a ticket to

Paris seemed to me simply a pleasant fantasy that became a conversational riff we could do in our sleep; reassuring and affectionate with no binding obligations on either side.

After a year or so of camping out with us, Lucius moved to Texas and inherited a substantial sum from a long-dead grandfather. Perhaps in order to prove that he was still a bohemian in spite of his newfound wealth, or perhaps simply to say thanks and I love you to a friend, he used part of that money to buy me a ticket to Paris.

When it arrived in the mail, I was amazed. It looked like an ordinary airplane ticket that might take me to Cleveland or Newark, but this was nothing of the kind. This was a ticket to my dreams. An acknowledgement of my right to be there, in Paris, as a writer. This was a ticket that would let me walk in the footsteps of Josephine Baker and Anais Nin and Bricktop. I held it in my hands and I knew I was ready, finally ready, so ready! But I also knew it was too late. Too many bombs in too many airports. Too many machine guns. Too many charges and countercharges and airstrikes and terrorists and threatening mantones from all sides of the globe. I cannot go to Paris because the world has gone berserk. Again.

There is no poetic ending to this story, although I tried hard to find one. There is only the fact that I'm too scared to make the trip and can't decide if I'm angrier at the state of the world, my own cowardice, or Lucius' lousy timing.

Observation

You are too quiet,
my daughter tells me.
It makes me
think you're angry.
I am thinking,
I tell her.

I am trying not to run.

Heading Home

Knowing all along a call like this would probably come some day does not make it any easier the day it does occur. I am not there to take it, so he must tell me the news. He worries that I am not prepared, tries to gauge my mood before he speaks.

I see in his face that something terrible has happened. Is the baby OK, I say, my mind filled with screeching tires and mangled limbs. Yes, yes, fine, he says and stops. Are you all right, I say, and touch his hand, trying to imagine what I will do if he does not say yes. It's your mother, he says, his eyes watching me, his voice wishing he could alter the message. Your mother is very sick.

His voice glides into the details: Date of check-in at a hospital I have never seen in a town I have never been to; what miracles we are expecting from doctors whose neatly lettered diplomas cannot make them gods; arrangements to be made for the trip home.

Guilt is packed in among my toothpaste and T-shirts and faded jeans. Remembering all the Christmases and springtimes and birthdays we were going to spend together but got too busy or too scared of airplanes or too bored with fourteen hour drives. Remembering the promised phone calls and letters that never quite got made or written.

My stepfather comes to meet my plane with tired eyes, our first real hug since childhood, and more details. She is doing well. The doctor says this or that, but never what we want most to hear, that it has all been a mistake and we can go home now, pick some green beans from the garden and fry some fish and play Leontyne Price and Billie Holiday records and laugh about how scared we were.

23

She seems so small in the hospital room where I first see her sleeping, although I know we are the same size. She sleeps fitfully with the drugs they have given her, and when she wakes and turns to me, I babble about novels I will write and movies I will make and the perfection of my child, her fourth granddaughter. And she smiles and sleeps again.

I watch her getting stronger, beginning to walk without wincing, doing what she is asked to do by these round-faced nurses who pat her hand and tell me I have a wonderful mother. And I nod and say yes, I know, while they gather their own set of details: temperature, color of urine, the movement of bowels. To distract her from these probing hands and watchful eyes, I tell my mother of worried friends who send their love, and she covers her mouth with a corner of the sheet like a small child and shakes her head, eyes brimming. No, don't tell me that, she says. I can't stand it when people worry about me.

We bring her home when her charts say that she is ready, settling her gently into the back seat, crawling over railroad tracks to avoid shaking her. She laughs at our concern, and we laugh with her, grateful to have her back.

But I am someone's mother, too; someone who calls daily to ask in a small voice when I am coming home, so I do not stay long. My mother will not go to the airport with me. We agree to play our parting scene in the privacy of her garden. We surprise ourselves and each other. We do not cry or clutch. I hug her gently and kiss her, and she tells me she is glad I came to take care of her. I tell her that if she will promise always to take care of me, I will promise always to take care of her. We shake hands to seal the bargain.

The plane is late and crowded, and the flight is bumpy enough so that I indulge the first-class flyer's prerogative and down two free drinks. There's a thunderstorm on our right, says the pilot.

Nothing to worry about, but quite a light show for you for the next couple of minutes.

He's right. The lightning flashes but fades quickly and leaves us hurtling through darkness. Heading home.

Zen And The Art Of Beetle Killing

I'm scared of beetles. There. It's out in the open. I confess.
It's not an easy thing to talk about publicly. I am, after all, a
modern, independent woman and confession of beetlephobia
conjures up undeniably retro-images of squealing, helpless
women that are not at all appealing to me. But the fact is, the
sight of a beetle scurrying across my kitchen floor is guaranteed
to make me drop everything and head for help. I think I may
even have squealed a time or two.

I used to call them waterbugs. In New Orleans, they call
them palmetto bugs. You know the kind. Big and black and
long feelers and fast runners and always come out around mid-
night when you didn't need to go into the kitchen anyway since
you'd had enough wine for one day, but you did, and now
you've seen it heading under the stove and you know it's there
and it's alive and if you don't get it killed you won't be able to
sleep for dreading that deep-night moment when your hand,
dangling over the side of the bed, feels the brush of those feelers
and the beetle is right there!

Now this may sound funny to you, but I know my very real
shame about it causes me to write in a far more jovial tone than
I have any right to use. Beetles are not funny to me. My two
closest male friends have both come to my house in the wee
hours to kill beetles, smile indulgently and then leave me to my
own devices. They have accepted these infrequent but urgent
requests as part of our friendship and while they aren't quite sure
why, they know the degree of my discomfort about beetles is
akin to how most people feel about being trapped in a small
room with a rabid Doberman and they indulge me accordingly.
The importance of this indulgence can be seen in the fact that

when I find myself listing one or the other's finer points, beetle killing is always on the list right alongside the fact that each one cooked breakfast for Angela Davis, but that is neither here nor there. I'm talking about beetles, not breakfast.

Beetles are really harmless, the exterminator said. They come indoors looking for food and water, he told me, just like we do. Well, not quite, I wanted to say. I don't crawl under screens and terrorize innocent people just because I'd like some leftover cheese sandwich and a bit of that Kool-Aid. Of course I didn't say that. Exterminators are not known for their sense of humor. Besides, I needed help closer to home. It came in the person of my 11 year old daughter.

I've tried to raise my daughter not to be scared of the things that terrorize me, at least the ones that scare me for no good reason. Things like death and cancer I figure are really scary and anybody who tries to reassure you about them is not operating in your best interests or is connected in some official way to the church. So, at first, my daughter did not share my fear of beetles. But then as she began to observe me, crazed with fear, she wondered if she shouldn't be afraid too and she began not to want to kill them, to run from them, and finally to tell me to call a man for help when we found one in her room just at bedtime.

I knew I was setting a bad example, but fear made me helpless. Then the other night my friend who just drove to Detroit and back with her two young sons was over and a beetle entered through the porch door, skittering to temporary refuge under the dining room table. I appealed to her. You drove 1,000 miles, I said. You're strong. Do my feet look any different from yours, she said, raising her eyebrows. And what could I say? It's not acceptable form to press a woman friend to kill a beetle. A man? I would have been home free, but there was no man around. So I took a deep breath, then my daughter spoke up. Do you want me to kill it, she said. I was so grateful, so amazed, so pleased that she had found a way around her fear and that I had not ruined her life by making her a permanent beetle-phobe that I said, I'll pay you ten bucks every time you kill one. Done, she said amazed at such unexpected generosity since cash is not our agreed upon form of barter for household tasks. We shook hands to seal the deal while the victim waved his feelers around and tried to be invisible under the table. My daughter grabbed a heavy book full of color prints of Alexander Calder's work, ran the beetle toward the porch door and dropped Calder on him with a thud. He died instantly. She was delighted. I was ecstatic.

Since then, she has killed two huge beetles fearlessly. I holler now when I see them, not from fear, but to get her attention: Hey, Deig! There's ten bucks in the kitchen waiting for you. And when I watch her stride toward her task, I am as proud of her as I have ever been.

The only problem is, it's getting pretty expensive and I think economics may triumph where self-admonitions to be a brave soldier had failed. Last time my daugher killed a beetle, I watched her carefully and just yesterday I moved Alexander Calder into the kitchen near the cookbooks. Somehow, I think he'd understand.

Selena's Poem

you will never
have this energy again.
it is a virgin's energy
that propels you forward.
the energy that comes
from sleeping with your
knees closed.

a dancer's flat foot grace,
your hair a braided tail
behind you,
you spend this last pure summer
laughing and learning how to kiss.

as a little girl,
you took my daughter wino-dancing,
the two of you so beautiful
in the park you charmed them
into being sober.

you will never
have this energy again.
this is the last pure summer
when all that fills you
is the shimmer of your dreams,
and the shiver of your schemes,
and the quiver
of your knees falling open,
your body yearning,
yearning upward,
in the darkness.

Four From That Summer: Atlanta, 1981

One: May

My daughter is six and knows the words to songs by Kool and the Gang and the pledge of allegiance to the flag. My daughter has a closely cropped afro like mine, filigreed golden earrings from South America, and makes collages with me on Sunday afternoons. She wears blue jeans with patches, light blue jogging shoes, pleated skirts and button-up sweaters, and, every Tuesday afternoon, a Brownie uniform with a cap that matches.

My daughter can read, write, do simple subtraction and speak a few words of Spanish. With no attempt at objectivity, I would describe her as an almost perfect child. She is also a *black* child, and at the present time, she is living under a state of siege in the City of Atlanta.

Since July, 1979, when the first body was found, until last week when the seventeenth was confirmed, the mystery and horror surrounding the murders of black Atlanta children have been mounting. Adults feel outraged, frightened, incredulous, angry, suspicious. Kids feel surprised.

"Why are they killing kids?" my daughter says, and it is impossible to answer. Explanations center on a sick mind. Someone who doesn't know what they are doing. Can't help it. Someone driven and desperate.

My daughter's eyes fight against the words. She is unwilling to admit to adult madness or to her own vulnerability. There is nothing in her six year old child's consciousness to account for random, calculated violence against her peers. It is like being a woman and first understanding what rape is.

A few days later, my daughter and I are deciding between hash browns and pancakes at the McDonald's drive-in window and she says, "What if we could carry guns?" "What?" I say. "Guns," she says, "kids could all have guns and then if somebody tries to make us get in a car, we could whip out the guns and say no! Leave us alone or we'll shoot you!"

A few days after that, she says: "We run home from the bus now." She is talking about herself and the children she walks home from school with; another little black girl, also age six, and two little black boys, ages eight and ten. They used to *walk* the block from the bus stop, examining dead possums in the street, singing the chants they learn on the bus to pass the distance, chasing each other, whispering and giggling and kicking rocks.

Now when they get off the bus, they join hands and run the block, arriving at home out of breath, panting, looking over their shoulders, poking each other, and feeling foolish at being so frightened of something they can't see or understand.

Being a black child in Atlanta now must be a little like being a Northern black person watching Bull Connor at work during the Sixties. We would sit in Detroit, or Chicago, or Philadelphia, and watch the Alabama police cracking heads, and feel for the first time a kind of vulnerability that settled on our chests like witch-trial stones and stayed there.

Except then we could do something. We could send money to Civil Rights groups, or march in the street, or read books about the "Revolution" and refuse to accept our second-classness by confronting those who would deny us.

My daughter has no money to send to anyone. The marches begin nowhere and end nowhere. There are no books about or-

ganizing to fight people who murder small children and there is
no way she can possibly refuse to accept her childness.

"I don't think it's a good idea for kids to carry guns," I tell
my daughter. "Guns are very complicated and kids might shoot
each other by mistake."

My daughter considers this and then speaks without looking
up from her lap. "Well," she says softly, "we wouldn't have to
use the bullets. Maybe we could just scare the people away
from us. We would promise to be real careful," she says.

And it is my turn to look away.

Two: June

(Letter to a friend just back from a bad month in New
Orleans)

what price cynicism?
in love and too jaded to write a love poem.
all victories difficult.
all gains constantly under threat of erosion.
everybody has a hungry heart.
dear kay:
my life in the bush of ghosts:
lunch at gabriel's restaurant with a political operative.
what do you hear, he says. politically, i mean.
adjusting glasses. smoking dark brown cigarettes
without inhaling.
scrambled tofu, i say, with green peppers and onions.
and white wine, i add, knowing he can afford it. this
is a campaign lunch after all.
well, not much, i say.

i don't do politics anymore.
i don't read the paper.
i don't go to city hall.
i hardly vote.
and if i can manage, i just generally don't give a damn.
see?

my life in the bush of ghosts:
New Orleans always seems like refuge until you turn on the
t.v. in the motel where Mark Essex went up on the roof and
demanded his stuff back and they are showing *Vixens* in living
color. Or until the junebugs walk up your arm while you sit
hunched over your typewriter as if the only difference between
flesh and furniture is temporary, with the distinction so tenuous
as to be inconsequential.

James Caan told *Rolling Stone* that he had lunch with Mar-
lon Brando and Brando said, Jim, whattya want more than any-
thing else in the world? And Caan reports that his answer was,
I'd like to be in love. And Brando said, yeah, me too

my life in the bush of ghosts:
A midnight phone call from L.A. tells me that Bob Marley's
cancer has spread everywhere and he has no more locks and no
more chances. My mother writes one page of determined cheer-
fulness to tell me the new medication isn't working and she will
start chemotherapy in two weeks and even though my stepfather
won't let her smoke dope, I consider asking a friend to get me a
couple of ounces of the best Hawaiian for old times' sake in case
she needs it.

the bushes are full of ghosts:

The wind is up outside and Peachtree Street traffic snakes toward a disco called "Animal Crackers" and they're pulling bodies from the river so fast my friends call from California/Indiana/Detroit/Mississippi and demand answers from *me*. They are incredulous/angry/frightened. My daughter suggests that maybe I should let my hair grow since some of the children are bigger than I am and she is afraid someone will think I am a boy.

the bushes are always full of ghosts:
New Orleans is a dream.
The wind makes Peachtree feel like a moor and I crane my neck, strain my eyes, searching for Heathcliff in the darkness.

Soon come.
Love,
P.

Three: July

It is billed as a benefit for the children's fund, but it's Michael Jackson at the Omni and the only relevant question is: how can one little Negro be so fine? He is beautiful and young and glitter pants and silver shoes and my daughter in my arms, eyes as round as the moon, holding her hands over her ears against the roaring of the crowd.

"This is the loudest noise I've ever heard," she says to me, cuddling closer. And I hold her and we sway and laugh and scream.

"Michael!" we say. "Oh, Michael!"

Now half past midnight, and home. Exhausted, I tack up the poster we have bought of the five Jackson brothers gazing at the camera with shirts open to the waist and hands on hips and tight jeans and they seem alive in our small room. They are a tangible presence with *heat*. I talk to the poster.

"Hi guys," I say. "Good concert!"

"Mom!" my daughter says, and laughs a little.

"Put on your nightgown," I say, but she stands still. Shy. Embarrassed. Eyes riveted to toenails.

"What's wrong," I say. Confused.

She looks up, flushed, and when I see her face, I know what it is. She cannot change in front of the poster boys. They are too real. Too present. Too wide-eyed and staring.

"Not in front of them?" I say, and she grins, sheepish and relieved, hiding her head against my stomach. "Yeah," she says. "They keep lookin' at me!"

"Want me to take them down?"

"Put them on another wall," she says.

I take them down, apologizing. "Sorry about this, Mike, but you guys gotta lighten up just a little bit okay? The kid is only seven!" And she laughs.

We tack them up over the ironing board, neutral territory, and tell them good night. She is yawning now, curled up in her Jacksons' tee shirt instead of a nightgown, and we laugh and she says, "I love you," and I say, "I love you too."

And she smiles again, asleep before she can reply.

Four: August

Twenty-eight dead and we began to share the same pictures. Explore the same theories. We decided it was genocide.

Drooling rednecks, consumed by hatred and evil.

35

Plotting in the hills. Stashing rifles in the trunks of their cars. Transporting ammunition in the backs of dirty pick-up trucks. Travelling in packs like mad dogs.

Sneaking into our community. Spying on us. Isolating our children. Waiting until they are vulnerable. Snatching them off the street. Snuffing the life out of them. Throwing their bodies in the woods. Sliding them into the river with a splash where they turn up downstream days later, swollen and stinking.

We wanted it to be one of Them. One of those we already know is after us. One of the ones we have already learned to watch out for.

We are not prepared for the Suspect–the Accused–to be one of our own. We are not ready to gaze at his picture on the front page and look into our own eyes, the eyes of our brothers/husbands/fathers/lovers/sons. We are not prepared for the madness to show itself this way. Not prepared for the hatred to turn inward, gnawing on itself as if it was possible to eat its way out, and still survive.

The arrest of the Suspect does not comfort or reassure us. "A scapegoat," we say to each other. "Pressure from the White House." "The governor made them do it, man. Don't you know anything? We become investigators, dismissing publicized evidence as inconclusive, circumstantial, unconvincing.

We still admonish our children to travel in groups and not to go with strangers. We still share the vision of the carload of Klansmen cruising our street, tracking our young manhood as if they were rabbits. We still close our eyes and shake our heads and look away from each other's faces when they flash the Suspect's picture on the nightly news.

It's just too close. Too familiar a face to be the Danger...to be the fear made flesh...and the flesh made fear...beating among us like a telltale heart.

But Where Are You Now?

I walk into Plaza Drugs and a tiny little kid is holding the phone at both ends and saying "Where are you now?" and, not getting the answer he's looking for, he waits a minute, frowns and says it again. "Yes, but where are you now?"

I figure the answer is none of my business, so I wander through the aisles until I find the fake fingernail glue my daughter had requested for those at-home-piled-up-in-the-bed-together-nights watching TV and eating any kinda junk food we want when she applies fake fingernails with the precision of a surgeon, paints them fire engine red or frosted pink and holds her hands out to see how they will look when she finally leaves 12 behind and becomes the woman both of us can already see coming to the fore.

At the cash register is the tiny kid's mother who hands her money to the bored clerk in the big earrings and leans over to tell the kid to hang up the phone and the kid frowns like the request is not only absurd but way out of line and turns his back slowly like he was moving underwater. "Yes," he says again into the receiver, "yes, but where are you now?"

Now I'm walking into the record store and they're playing new music by the B-52's and the lead singer who once sang the immortal lines, "Why don't you dance with me?/I'm not no Limburger?" back in the group's glory days when Athens, Georgia, was famous for five minutes for something other than football and frat parties, was yodeling about wanting a man to move in and share expenses and do the dishes and help out around the house. Interesting idea, but not my style. I stop at the first bin that catches my eye and there are Muddy Waters and Howlin' Wolf on sale for $5.99 apiece and some Johnny or Edgar Winter albums and I can't remember which one of them is which or why and then the clerk takes off the B-52's and suddenly the store is full of rich, black African male voices singing harmonies that make you know how close Harlem is to Capetown and Detroit to Johannesburg. "Homeless," they are singing, "Moonlight sleeping on a midnight lake." And their voices are so full of longing for things that cannot be said but must be sung that I am drawn to the sound as if I had been searching for it all along.

"It's Paul Simon," says the clerk, grinning at my surprise and handing me the album jacket to prove it. Seems Paul heard some South African popular musicians and was drawn to them just like I was, although probably for different reasons. "Strong wind," they are singing now. "Many dead tonight, it could be you." And I look at little New York Paul Simon, pensive and a little self-conscious on the album cover and I plunk down my seven bucks so I can take these voices home on tape and listen closer and try to figure out what Paul is up to.

"Oh, god," says my daughter when I walk into the beauty parlor and show her the tape. "That Al song is on there! Everybody at school keeps singing it and I hate it! Don't play it," she says and tosses her head as the smiling beautician clacks the curling iron around her ears in an expert rhythm as familiar to me as any I know.

There is a man who appears to be drunk curled up on the sidewalk on the other side of the plate glass window from where I sit down on an obscenely soft beauty shop sofa to wait for my daughter and listen to Paul Simon singing sweetly tentative harmonies through my Walkman: "I can call you Betty/and Betty when you call me/you can call me Al." I like it, my daughter's opinion notwithstanding, and I turn it up louder when the police arrive to wake the sleeping man so that when he raises up on one bare elbow and snarls indignantly at the bored police officer I can't hear anything but the music.

My daughter materializes in front of me, smiling, and I can't help gently placing the earphones on her newly coiffed head. "Your favorite song," I say, and Paul is singing, "If you'll be my body guard/I can be your long lost pal/I can call you Betty/and Betty when you call me/ you can call me..."

"Mommy!" says my daughter, carefully removing the earphones and pursing her lips self-righteously. "That's not funny."

But then she indulges me with a smile because she knows it sometimes makes me nervous when I see her looking so grown since she used to be my little baby girl. I let her have the umbrella as we run through the early evening downpour since my close-cut hair is unaffected by rain and humidity and because I like the way it feels when it is raining this hard and the drops go right through to my scalp in the way that my mother said would give me pneumonia, but hasn't yet. And we fall into the car out of breath giggling at nothing in particular and I feel so happy I almost want to cry because this feeling never lasts as long as I want it to no matter how many times I ask the question, "Yes, but where are you now?" But for this moment, it doesn't matter. We are here together and we love each other and we've got enough money to eat out so somebody else can do the dishes and all the things that drive us crazy won't be back until morning. Who could ask for anything more?

My Daughter Picks The One With The Sky In It

(for Deignan at 14)

The presence of O'Keefe is tangible
in my house
and that is by design.
Needing still more,
I find a portfolio of prints
and hurry hugging home.

We will each pick one.

I lay them out before her.
Peaceful brown adobe house
and patriotic skull head.
I choose the one that pretends to be
a purple orchid.
My daughter picks the one
with the sky in it.

Remembering Georgia O'Keefe

I am trying to remember when Georgia O'Keefe first invaded my imagination. I think it was somewhere around 1979 or 1980 during that amazingly manic moment that occurs as you somehow do the unthinkable and turn thirty. I had been aware of her as A Significant American Painter, but she had simply existed at the fringes of my consciousness as a name I had learned in Art Appreciation. Until I saw her naked.

I had seen her before, fully clothed. A small woman, already in her eighties by then, always wearing black and white and a rather grim expression, but she made little impression on me. I remember thinking that she had a certain prim straightness of spine that reminded me of my grandmother.

There was nothing in any of these fleeting impressions, however, to prepare me for the sight of Georgia O'Keefe naked. I was wandering through the gift shop at the local museum and there was a large book of photographs. "Georgia O'Keefe by Alfred Stieglitz" was all it said. If O'Keefe had barely penetrated my brain, Stieglitz was nowhere to be found on the landscape. Still, the small photograph of her on the front cover intrigued me, all hands and eyes and turned up collar, so I flipped open the book and there she was. She was standing in front of a lace curtain, and her body was so unexpectedly voluptuous and her pose so absolutely unselfconscious that I couldn't take my eyes off of her. A Significant American Painter? Stark naked for all the world to see? What was going on here?

The next few pages were no less of a shock to my system. O'Keefe seated with her legs sprawled. O'Keefe with only a thin robe falling over her shoulders and her nipples puckered

41

with passion or a sudden chill. What kind of woman was this Georgia O'Keefe, and who in the hell was Alfred Stieglitz?

The rest of the book showed the small woman in black, often hooded, almost always somber, but I was on to her protective coloration now. Her fearless exposing of her body had made it possible for me to look into her eyes. I bought the book and took it home to study it–to study her.

I moved from the photographs to a biography of her life and I began to understand her painting, her struggle to be an artist and a free woman, the intensity of her thirty-year relationship with Stieglitz as her lover, her husband, her colleague, her friend, her tormentor.

I think it was her courage that initially inspired me the most. Perhaps it was her discipline and commitment to her work; her willingness to sacrifice to get it done. Perhaps it was the fact that in spite of all the struggles, her paintings emerged with a confident sensuality that drew me to them with a force I had not experienced before. I sought out exhibition catalogues and posters, experiencing for the first time the frustration of the art lover in the face of inadequate prints unable to capture the real color, the real line, the real life.

But one day on a trip to Washington, D.C., I escaped a meeting and fled to the East Wing of the National Gallery of Art. After a few inquiries to helpful guards who seemed used to passionate pilgrims inquiring about the whereabouts of O'Keefe's work, I found myself standing in front of my first real O'Keefe flower. I don't remember what kind it was, but it was dark purple and deep violet and unequivocally female and you could look down so deep into its swirling depths that you felt as if you might fall in, or might want to.

I stood there long enough to attract the attention of a guard who positioned himself discreetly nearby to discourage whatever demonstration of affection I might have been contemplating. He needn't have worried. I didn't want to touch it. I wanted to be it —all mystery and mauve; all womanhood and wildness, stamens and stillness.

Georgia O'Keefe died a few weeks after I saw that flower and my mourning sent me back to Stieglitz' photographs. In those pictures, as in her own paintings, she remains vital and alive and as seductive as her oversized flowers, inviting you down to the places where you've never been before except in dreams. For her willingness to take that journey, I raise my glass and wish her goddess-speed and safe passage to the other side. Sending flowers would simply be redundant.

Bus Trip

When we were little, my sister would walk ahead of me on the street after it rained and fearlessly kick the drowning worms out of my path. At twenty-two, she packed a knapsack and a box of watercolors and set off for Berkeley on a Trailways bus. And at thirty-four, she has four daughters, aged two to ten, and lives on a farm in rural Mississippi.

I say all that only to show that my sister is not what you would call fainthearted and to help you understand my concern when she called me from the bus station last week to tell me she had arrived and then dropped her voice to a whisper.

"Pearl," she said, "something terrible happened. Or could have happened. Almost happened."

I heard my voice drop an octave or two like it always does when more than anything else, I am terrified of not sounding absolutely calm.

"Are you alright?"

"I'm fine," she reassures me. "Come and get me."

I rush into the bus station, my voice still doing its Marlene Dietrich imitation, toss her bags into the car and turn toward home. And this is what my sister said:

Around 3:30 a.m., she had gotten off the bus somewhere in the wilds of Alabama. The bus driver didn't see her, and after he got his cup of coffee, he hissed the doors closed and headed the bus back out onto the dark road toward Birmingham. When my sister came out of the Ladies Room, there was no one around but the waitress dozing behind the counter, and a middle-aged man in overalls drinking coffee with a bible sitting on the counter next to him. My sister freaked.

The waitress woke up long enough to tell her that there wouldn't be another bus until nine o'clock the next morning. My sister contemplated six hours of waiting with something less than complete enthusiasm. The man with the bible excused himself for eavesdropping and said he was going in that direction to visit his daughter in the hospital and would be happy to give my sister a ride up the road so she could flag the bus down and get on with her trip.

My sister contemplated the man's face. Lined and weather-beaten, it seemed, nonetheless, harmless enough. None of the secret rapist or crazed killer lurking behind the eyes. And, she scolded herself, he's carrying a bible, for goodness sake! How safe can you be?

The next six hours loomed large. She accepted the ride.

"When we hit the highway he realized I was nervous," my sister said, "so he started up a conversation to put me at ease." "Well," he said, "where you from?" When I told him Mississippi, he said, "That's a great state! I've got a lot of good friends in Mississippi. I'm a member of the Klan, you know, and we've got a lot of movement going on over there."

He spoke proudly, reaching into his wallet to produce his membership card to show my sister.

Perhaps in reciting her distinguishing characteristics, I should have noted that my sister is, like most of my southern bred family, a very light-skinned black American. We are sometimes mistaken for white, but since we aren't trying to "pass" we learn early to correct such cases of mistaken identity with as little embarrassment as possible on both sides. But nothing had prepared my sister for a head-on face-off with a card carrying member of the Ku Klux Klan.

My sister's ride had simply picked her up thinking she was a white lady in distress, and had no idea that he was discussing his Klan membership with a terrified "blue vein" who at that

45

moment was trying to throw race pride aside and concentrate on, as my sister said, "looking as white as possible."

When they got to the bus, my sister's ride did indeed flag it over and even got out to speak a few strong words to the driver about leaving this good lady back at the last stop. As they were about to pull off, he tipped his cap to my sister and waved a friendly good-bye.

The upshot of all this is difficult to say. Certainly it is not simply a question of the difficulties of being a hybrid in a society that encourages more straightforward definitions. Certainly it is more than a minor adventure in an otherwise uneventful trip from Jackson, Mississippi to Atlanta, Georgia. It can't be just a short story in which the waitress dozes and the Klansman has a bible on the counter when his character is first introduced.

But maybe that's all it is. Or maybe it's the parable of the Good Samaritan, southern style. Perhaps it is The Emperor's New Clothes, once removed.

But I guess it doesn't matter. My sister and I had a great visit. We caught up on all the old news, and tried to see into the future. And when she got ready to go back and decided to cash in the other half of that round trip bus ticket and take a plane, I wasn't even surprised.

At The Warwick Hotel

At the Warwick Hotel,
the desk clerk drinks,
the waitresses play the numbers
and they lock the door at midnight.
Late arrivals are greeted
with minor curiosity
and a blast of gin.

Aretha On The Waterfront

It was Saturday night and we were watching the late night movies presentation of *On the Waterfront* with Marlon Brando and Eva Marie Saint. My father and I had watched this movie together at least fifteen times before my twelfth birthday and we often spoke the lines just before the actors or right with them. Both of us did this frequently so neither one of us reprimanded the other for it in the way of those who like to watch their movies from a distance rather than participate in them.

This was, and is, a family trait that often shocks outsiders the first time they sit down with a room full of Cleages to look at a movie or a television show or a particularly obnoxious commercial. We talk over, under, around, and through it all, volume increasing as the number of participants in the discussion increases until the moment where nothing can be heard except my Uncle Louis snickering at his own wit and coughing loudly as he lights his 45th cigarette of the day from the glowing tip of the 44th one and declares the entire thing a waste of good film stock and who ever told that peckerwood he could act anyway? And then my grandmother would shush us all as if she was really trying to listen and as soon as everybody got quiet out of respect for her age and rank, she herself would let loose with a comment like "why is she wearing that awful dress?" and set off another round of talking, joking, laughing, and generally poking fun at everything flickering on the screen before us.

I always thought the comments from outside the small box were more amusing than the ones coming from the screen, but that is, of course, as much a matter of habit as of opinion. In any case, my father and I were alone as we often

were on Saturday nights and we could indulge this habit with
no fear of being shushed for disturbing the peace. We had al-
ready been through the scene where Marlon Brando, as
Terry Malloy, and Rod Steiger, as Charlie the Gent, discuss
Steiger's part in ruining Marlon's boxing career, and in ef-
fect his life, by making him take a fall to cover some bets
made by the consummate bad guy, Johnny Friendly who
sported a moniker so far from the truth as to be in the realm of
the ludicrous, and we were barreling along toward the mo-
ment when Marlon desperately beats on Eva's door trying to
explain to her that he didn't know that the bad guys were
going to kill her brother when he lured him up on the roof, and
the slip-clad Eva tells him to go away, she never wants to see
him again, but he refuses to take no for an answer, breaks in
the rickety door, and faces her with the classic palms-up
gesture of supplication.

"You gotta talk to me," he says. "You love me!"

"I didn't say I didn't love you," she shouts at him. "I said get
out!"

At which point he grabs her in a Marlon Brando hug and she
thrashes around, beating him ineffectually about the head and
shoulders for a few moments before her fists do the famous Hol-
lywood-leading-lady transformation and stop hitting him so she
can hug him tightly and return his embrace. This always hap-
pens in the movies. Even Scarlett O'Hara wakes up smiling and
docile after being subjected to perhaps the most famous rape in
motion picture history at the hands of Rhett Butler.

But that's neither here nor there. The point is, my father
had carried the bulk of the load during the back seat of the car
Charlie-you-ruined-my-life-by-making-me-throw-that-fight
scene and I was ready to do Eva with equal style and meti-
culous care when the phone rang. It was already after mid-

night, but my father didn't even look at his watch. People called his house at all hours of the day and night. Sometimes church members with a problem, sometimes radicals with an idea, sometimes family with an update, and sometimes heavily breathing men who held the phone for several minutes and then mumbled something about what happens to smart-ass niggas who don't know enough to shut the hell up about civil rights, and then hung up. My father took these calls with equal aplomb and when he tired of them, he simply took his phone off the hook and dropped it in a dresser drawer, at which point some more determined callers, after getting two hours of busy signals, would try the operator to report trouble on the line and be told by the bored operator that Rev. Cleage's phone was on "time service."

But this night, it rang and my father left me alone to my big scene and went to answer. He was gone for several minutes, long enough to miss my scene, but not long enough to miss the really scary shot of Charlie the Gent hung up on the meat hook in the alley as a warning to anybody who thought loyalty to family could take precedence over loyalty to Johnny Friendly. When he came back his expression was a mixture of about ten things at one time and his eyes were sad.

"Who was it," I said.

"Aretha Franklin," he said.

I waited for further comment, but my father just kept staring in the general direction of the TV and sort of shook his head. Now I knew my father and Aretha's father were well acquainted, although I wouldn't call them friends exactly. Rev. C. L. Franklin's church was located on the other side of Linwood about six blocks down the street from my father's church in Detroit and we often passed it on the way to Sunday services. Rev. Franklin had a large and enthusiastic congregation of almost 2,000 members and he guided his flock with a superb blend of style and slickness that guaranteed a majority of the members were female and would contribute regularly and with enthusiasm to everything from The Missionary Board to the Pastor's Special Fund.

In the pulpit, Rev. Franklin favored flowing robes with gold or red trim, depending on the time of year. For street wear, he leaned toward grey sharkskin suits and diamond stickpins and a low-rise process waved carefully close to his amazingly round skull. My father and Rev. Franklin had sometimes found themselves on the same side of big general issues, like a visit to the town by Rev. Martin Luther King, Jr. But most often they maintained a cordial respect for each other and went their separate ways. I never even knew my father knew Aretha.

"I don't," he said, in response to the question I had to ask after it looked like he was just going to get back into the movie with no further explanation about the phone call.

"I've never even met her," he said.

"Well, what did she want?" I asked, wondering if I was going to have to drag the story out of him or if he would finally break down and tell me.

"She wanted to know if I had Muhammad Ali's telephone number," he said, turning to look at me, and frowning slightly.

"Why?" I asked, visions of Aretha Franklin with a crush on the fine-as-wine heavyweight champion already dancing in my head.

"Her husband keeps beating her up and she wants to call Muhammad Ali and ask him if he will come over and kick her old man's butt for her." My father shook his head and turned back to the movie. "I told her I was sorry but I didn't have his number. And she said, well, okay, she guessed she could handle it. And she hung up."

Years later, when her stormy marriage to Ted White had finally broken up for the last time, Aretha released a mediocre album of lackluster songs that sounded like she had recorded them underwater. Her picture on the front showed a newly slim, suddenly blond woman trying to smile brightly for the camera, but her eyes had the on-the-edge-of-panic look animals have when they are frozen in your headlights that moment you have to decide whether to swerve or to hit them.

My father and I listened to the record once and took it off, in much the same way I remember my mother sadly replacing a Billie Holiday album in its cover after one quick listen through when Lady Day spent as much time wheezing and coughing as she did trying to croak out a song through a throat constricted by pain and dope and bad men and bad liquor. My father shook his head.

"That doesn't even sound like Aretha," he said.

"She looks pretty good," I said, clutching at straws. My father looked at me like I had lost my mind then realized that I saw and heard it too, but was more prone to denial then he was. He smiled at me gently.

"The really sad thing," he said, "is that she was singing better when she was with that dude who used to beat her up all the time."

"Well," I said, "I'd rather that she never sing another note than have to go through that."

My father looked at me again and shrugged. "Yeah," he said. "I guess...but she usta really sing."

She usta really sing.

Them Changes

Before he fled the Renaissance, my friend Charlie O used to say "your eyes can't see what your mind can't comprehend." This statement was invariably accompanied by a slow shake of the head and a pained rolling of the eyes to indicate that being the only conscious member of the group was quite a burden since the rest of us didn't even have the decency or good manners not to snicker, which is what we used to do regularly when O intoned this catchall explanation of the human condition. But I'm beginning to think he knew what he was talking about.

The problem is that the converse, or the reverse, or the vice versa, is also true. That is, once your mind can comprehend the awful It, your eyes cannot help but see It. Everywhere. Which is, of course, what should happen and is probably the fact that gave rise to cliches like "older and wiser" and "youth is wasted on the young." And I do want to see more clearly, understand more completely and to finally, arduously, arrive at the state of grace that only comes with seeing The Whole Picture. I know all that.

But I had been thinking that The Whole Picture was going to come into focus like a movie. I had visions of the results of my efforts emerging slowly but steadily from a foggy, blob-filled gray into a sharply etched, full-color extravaganza. But slowly. Slowly.

I was wrong. It isn't working like that at all. It's more like a jigsaw puzzle. Some parts of it are really clear and other parts are just shades of blue with something brown in the corner that's not a tree, but doesn't look like furniture either. Then all of a sudden, you see a little more of It and It isn't a tree or furniture or love or anything sweet at all. It's something terrible that jumps out everywhere in everything on everybody even when you wish it wouldn't, and how many more pieces before you see It all anyway?

This week begins with a story of a young girl raped and brutally murdered, her body left in her own apartment for her mother to find when she got home. Another piece. The next day the newspapers report a rapist who drags women into the woods, beats and rapes them and then cuts out their right eyes before leaving them for dead and moving on to the next one. Another piece. The next day two women are killed by their husbands before their divorces come through and their bodies left in cars and on the street in front of convenience stores for the police to find. Another piece. The week ends with a young girl run off the road and shot by a strange man who wanted to rob her or worse and wouldn't take no for an answer. Another piece.

I see the pieces everywhere. It is as if all of a sudden we are under siege, although no war has been declared. It is getting harder and harder to tell the difference between the danger and the protection from the danger. I am beginning to see what sexism really means and I can't stand it or stand for it, no matter what my eyes can see and my mind, however much it struggles not to, continues to comprehend.

So I try to understand and analyze. I stroke my daughter's cheek while she is sleeping and meet her at the bus stop when she comes from school so she won't have to walk two blocks alone. The last time she tried it, a car full of men followed her down the street, sucking their teeth and offering a free ride home. I stop myself when I start snapping at the men I love and hope I don't start crying on the telephone at midnight. I wish my mother was here so I could ask her to explain. As if she could. As if anybody could.

And how much do my eyes have to see for my mind to comprehend and know what to do and to whom and toward what end? And is it absolutely necessary for me to be blinded by the light before I can find the words to say what we have become, marooned in the madness of this place that is determined to destroy us and has finally found the way?

And where is the O when I need him?

Life In Wartime

I just moved back into the black community after a five-year self-imposed, post-divorce exile during which I wandered up and down Peachtree Street, living in a series of bohemian apartments, trying to be invisible. I liked living on Peachtree Street. I liked being within safe walking distance of so many theaters where somebody was always showing something I liked. I liked the cafes with outdoor seating and candles on the tables. I liked being able to sit on the front steps of my building without being scared. And I liked the grocery stores.

But I got lonesome. I missed the faces that look like me even when they're angry or crazy or sad, so I abandoned Peachtree Street and bought a house on a busy corner where the buses run 22 out of 24 hours and the only white faces you see are coming to collect insurance payments or to spray for roaches. And I love my neighborhood. I love that little barbecue stand at the fork in the road where one street goes to Ingrid's house and one goes to Walt's and they have the best ribs and chicken that melts in your mouth. I love that bakery near our neighborhood park where the proprietor is an enthusiastic Christian who sells her "blessed" baked goods and throws in a few minutes of her optimistic world view at no extra charge. I love those wide-eyed kids who come and ring the doorbell and ask if my daughter can come out and then look so crestfallen if she can't that I almost throw caution and homework to the wind and let her go. Most of all, there's a sense of being home again; of being back in the bosom of my extended family and finally feeling that all is forgiven or understood or never was the deal anyway.

It was probably this last which distracted me so thoroughly that I traded in my cynical black Raybans for a pair of wire-rimmed rose colored glasses. To my mind, my southwest Atlanta neighborhood was as close to Paradise as I could stand to be at the moment. But my friend David, a recent emigre from Texas, didn't see it that way. "Have you been to the grocery store lately?" he said, angrily unpacking one of several bulging sacks he had just carried in. His fiancée was preparing lasagna for a pack of us and they had been out shopping. "It's terrible," he said. "Don't you see how terrible it is?"

"Of course I see it," I heard myself say in that obnoxiously condescending tone that implies older and wiser. "I told you to go across town." His fiancée quickly assured me that they had done so after trying our neighborhood A&P, but my friend would have none of it. "That's not the point," he said. "Why should we have to go so far? Why are all the grocery stores in this neighborhood so bad?"

I opened my mouth to counsel taking the long view and the freeway headed north when I stopped. I knew exactly what he was talking about. Withered produce, poorly stocked shelves, overcrowded aisles, dirty floors, dim lighting, limited selections in every category and too-close-to-purple-for-comfort meat. He was used to grocery stores that looked like the ones I got used to when I was living on Peachtree Street. Spanking new grocery stores where the fish have their own tanks, the spice rack has three kinds of vanilla beans, the bakery has fresh bagels daily, the meat is pink and tender and the produce is so fresh it whistles. Grocery stores with bright lights, floors you could eat off of and smiling young men and women whose job is to put your parcels in your car and wish you a good day. There are no grocery stores like that in my neighborhood. There are no grocery stores like that in any black community I've ever been in, not because we don't like to eat well, but because one of the mysterious things about urban American racism is that major food chains consistently operate their stores in black areas using a different, much lower standard than they apply in white neighborhoods. Although the same can be said of some chain stores in poor white areas, it can be said of every chain store in every black area, economic status notwithstanding.

My friend's outrage made me realize that I had accepted the poor quality of the grocery store in my new neighborhood as an unchangeable fact of life. I had simply continued to shop in my old neighborhood rather than settle for what was being provided for my neighbors. I had looked the other way and made the necessary adjustments for the simple reason that it was easier. It is exhausting to think about racism all the damn time.

But my friend was right and I admitted he had a point and offered to join him in picketing the grocery store giant of his choice. He wasn't through fussing yet, though, and as every good community organizer knows, you can't plot strategy until the fussing is all out. But just as he was winding down, the lasagna came out of the oven and the others swarmed into the kitchen and everybody was laughing and eating and feeling good and it seemed a shame to bring it up and spoil the meal. So I didn't.

My Mother Hated Being Poor

(Xmas, 1964)

My mother hated being poor at Christmas. She hated being poor anytime, but Christmas just seemed to add insult to injury. It increased her irritation geometrically. Her parents had come through the depression with barely a ripple in their household even when Mr. Ford laid my grandfather off. "I told Shell when we first got married," my grandmother told my mother, and whenever she told the story my mother told me, "I told Shell if you let me handle all the money, whenever you need some, you'll have some." And he did, and she did, and "We never were hungry," my mother would say.

And we weren't hungry this Christmas. We had a turkey. Which was the problem. My mother was cooking the turkey in the temporary stand-up oven we were using because our real oven had broken and we didn't have money enough to get it fixed. My Uncle Louis had this stand-up thing in the garage for a long time and when my stepfather asked him if we could borrow it he said sure.

My mother hated borrowing anything from her in-laws, but she had to have something to cook the turkey in and this thing was the only possibility unless she just wasn't going to cook at all this Christmas, and that didn't seem to be an option, although I don't remember why we weren't going to one grandmother or another. But we weren't. We were eating at home as soon as the slower-than-it-should-be-stand-up-oven finished cooking the turkey which my mother had expected out and on the table almost an hour ago, but it wasn't quite done yet, and there is nothing worse than poultry with blood on the bone. So we were waiting.

59

The other food was ready and beginning to wilt just a little. There was a second skin on the gravy and the green beans were getting a little mushy. But mostly my mother was getting mad about being poor.

She was probably even madder, although I didn't understand this then, because she knew why we were poor and she couldn't argue it. She knew she had married into a family of people who spent their lives fighting white folks. Period. Not the most lucrative life's work in America.

The latest family venture was the publishing of a radical weekly tabloid which was single-handedly raising the level of discussion in barber shops and pool rooms all over Detroit.

My mother shared the commitment and loved the paper, but it was, of course, making no money, and the press she and my stepfather had purchased to print it on was a huge West German monstrosity that was sucking money out the door as fast as it spit out the printed pink sheets of the paper. My mother was in the terrible position of loving the idea, and being an integral part of the struggle, but wishing the sacrifice wasn't always so present and so personal.

And the turkey was taking forever. Finally, she tested it one more time and it seemed to be ready. She lifted it out carefully and my sister and I breathed in the wonderful aroma of Christmas dinner. The turkey was perfectly brown. The homemade dressing was spilling out of one end smelling of celery and sage and the drum sticks were tucked demurely at the other. My mother smiled and relaxed for the first time that day, and then she saw the spot.

On the turkey's right breast, there was a blue spot about the size of a quarter. It was an ominous, metallic blue for a turkey breast. My mother touched it with her finger and frowned. She lifted the top of the freestanding oven, looked on the inside of it, and there was a strange little twisted wire thing sticking out that

60

had obviously laid on our turkey as it cooked and deposited some metallic junk on one of its beautiful breasts.

My sister and I looked at each other and then at my mother as she carefully, too carefully, laid the top down on the stove and called my stepfather. What she wanted to tell him was that the turkey was obviously metal poisoned by the strange wire; that we couldn't possibly eat it since we would all die instantly; that she was sorry but she was going to have to throw the whole thing away. What she wanted to *imply* was that it was his fault for not making enough money to fix her oven.

My stepfather, having walked into a hornet's nest completely unsuspecting, heard all this, looked from my mother's angry face to the almost perfect bird and made a grave error. He laughed. My mother pursed her lips in the way that runs through generations of women in my family and stalked out of the room. My stepfather looked at my sister and me and grinned, but we were having none of it. We eased out of the room and left him alone with the bird.

My mother returned in a few minutes with a Kleenex clutched in her hand and her sunglasses on. This meant she had been upstairs crying and didn't want us to know it. I always wondered what could have been any more obvious than sudden sunglasses at five in the afternoon, inside the house, but it was none of my business.

We could hear them arguing quietly in the kitchen. My mother was determined to throw the tainted turkey out and my stepfather was trying to remain rational and save his Christmas dinner. The phone rang and my stepfather left the kitchen for a minute to answer it. By the time he got back, my mother was coming up the snow-covered back steps brushing off her hands and the turkey was lying in the garbage can behind our house.

"You're crazy," my stepfather said, amazed. "I'm not going to kill my family just because we don't have money enough to

61

fix a damn stove," said my mother. "That turkey wouldn't have killed anybody," said my stepfather in the deadly calm voice of someone determined not to argue but just as determined not to take a single step backward. "I ate a piece while you were out of the kitchen, and I'm just fine."

And he was. He never even threw up, or got diarrhea, or botulism, or any of the other ills my mother had predicted. And I'm sure she was glad although she probably wouldn't have objected to a stomach cramp or two. We even ended up with a Christmas care package from my grandmother delivered by my two grinning uncles who had heard the story and came to try to help us save our Christmas, or what was left of it.

But my mother would not be comforted. She was still so mad she couldn't even appreciate the foil-covered plate of turkey and dressing my uncles unwrapped and offered with the perfect dose of don't-take-it-all-so-serious good humor. So they shrugged and smiled, backed away, and waited for my stepfather to redeem himself although everybody knew he wasn't really the villain even if he had laughed when he should have shared her tears. My mother knew it too, but she did not seem to be in the mood for redemption, demanding as it does confession and forgiveness. Even though she understood everything, she didn't have to like it. Especially at Christmas.

Merry Xmas, Baby

When you come from a family as high-strung as mine, holidays take a life of their own. Due to the excitement brought on by what my grandmother used to call the high quantity of salt in the air, there was always the potential for major disasters resulting in towering rages, disappointments of mythical proportions, joy teetering perilously close to complete hysteria, and egos so exposed and inevitably battered that it took until next Christmas for things to settle down so that they could begin all over again.

It made for exciting times around the holiday table. But madness takes its toll, and by the time we gathered for a toast of New Year's egg nog, I was wary and exhausted. Not sure if my Uncle Louis was still speaking to my father or if Aunt Gladys was still mad at Aunt Barbara or if my mother was mad at my grandmother yet. I remembered vowing as a child that if I ever got out into the world and could control such things, I would never allow holidays to dominate months of my life through sheer force of remembered and anticipated stress.

And I was as good as my word. When I got out on my own, I gave holidays a wide berth. I stayed home as much as I could, accepted invitations to dinner rarely and went to the movies a lot. Better safe than sorry. I didn't even have a tree for the first three years I lived alone. I refused to cook turkey on Thanksgiving and gave presents only to my daughter and the few of my close friends who took it personally when I seemed to forget that this was a time for exchange of gifts.

But then one year I found myself wanting to acknowledge Christmas. I wanted to decorate something, string a few lights, drink egg nog in front of a fireplace. But I refused...for a moment. Then I remembered that this wasn't a principle stand, but a relief of stress stand, and figured I should go with the flow. I got a Christmas tree and I liked it. A lot. So far, so good. The next year, I decided to have friends over when a bunch of us found ourselves without plans for Christmas dinner and with that weird guilt that says if anybody loved you at all you would have someplace to go for Christmas dinner. They all came and we lit candles and set a place for Nelson Mandela and held hands and said thank you. And it was the nicest Christmas dinner I've ever had. I did it last year too and it was even better because we were all one year older and appreciated each other one year more.

So, I had managed to wrestle my childhood memories into submission and I had Christmas back. Then I got cocky. I started looking forward to it. I wanted Thanksgiving to hurry up and come so I could buy my tree and set it up. I wanted to buy presents and wrap them and hand out candy canes and cook turkey and dressing and giggle in the light from the Christmas tree when it was real late with the jazz station playing all that slow music for people who still like to make love with the radio on. I was ready! But it didn't feel like Christmas yet and I was getting impatient, which is, of course, the best way to bring on stress—exactly what I was trying to avoid in the first place. I thought I had blown it and been banished back to square one.

Until this morning. I was cruising through the morning rush hour traffic and all of a sudden, Otis Redding was on the radio singing "Merry Christmas, Baby" and his voice filled the car with such happy holiday black mannishness that I started grinning in spite of myself. This is the anniversary of Otis Redding's death the deejay had told me a minute ago and it made me just a little sad, but now here he was singing "Merry Christmas, Baby" in the kind of sweet man voice that makes you know he's going to be that way all the way 'til New Year's and hold you close and drag the tree in and laugh and go to the midnight services on Christmas

Eve even though that isn't usually his thing and light a candle and put his arm around your shoulder when you cry just a little because you're all there together and this year we'll set a place for Sweet Otis and all of a sudden it feels like Christmas!

So I breathed a sigh of relief that I hadn't spoiled my Christmas before it even got started good. And I sent a silent thank you to Otis telling him Merry Christmas and asking him to give my best to the Bar-Kays, wherever they might be.

Christmas, 1981

Last year, we spent it together, me and him. We thought it was important to the kid. We thought we could make her think it meant something for us to be sitting there, opening presents and taking snapshots.

I spent the night there, in the house where I used to live. And Christmas morning, I started smoking dope before it was ten o'clock. I had an excuse, though. I always cook better, I told him, when I'm high. Listening to loud music. Laughing with people who respond to questions like "Is it too early to start smoking?" by saying "It's midnight somewhere," and rolling another joint. I told him I thought sure he remembered that.

The thing is, there weren't any people around talking and laughing and playing music too loud to suit the neighbors. There wasn't anybody there Christmas, nor was anybody expected, except me and him and the kid.

This year, I'm gonna have my own tree at my own place. The kid suggested it and it seemed like a good idea, especially since the whole scene last year was about trying to give her what we thought she was supposed to have.

I think I used to like Christmas. I know I've always liked Christmas trees. The way they smell. The way they shed. The way you have to crawl under them to get water into that weird little three-legged tree stand. I remember how the yearly appearance of that stand always generated serious discussion about its ability to hold up anything, and how it always came through like a champ once the screws were twisted in right.

I don't know about the ornaments yet. We didn't split them up since the last year we spent Christmas together, like

I told you. The decorations aren't that important to me. Most of them anyway. I'd kind of like to have some of the ones we bought in that little shop in Columbia. The painted ones that are made out of hard bread dough. Little bread dough Joseph and Mary and three little bread dough wiseman, carrying their little bread dough coffers of gold, and frankincense and myrrh.

The shop where we bought them had a wall covered with nothing else. Little wreaths. Angels. Assorted shepherds. Lambs. Oxen. The Christ child in his little bread dough swaddling clothes. When we paid for our ornaments, the man behind the counter wished us a smiling "Feliz Navidad" and asked if we would like to buy some cocaine. We said no, thanks. But there was a sweetness and an ease in his voice that appealed to me. I liked to remember it when I used to hang the little shepherd and dust off the baby Jesus.

After last Christmas, I hooked up for awhile with a man who wore a small pistol strapped under his arm. He was a gambler who liked to play Miles Davis tapes when we made love. Sometimes he had dice in his left breast pocket. Sometimes he carried a marked deck of cards.

When he sat down with me on the edge of the bed, he would remove his shoes and his shirt, and then unbuckle the holster. He would hang it on the brass bed behind us with his vest. Sometimes I could see the little pistol in the holster above my head. It seemed dangerous swinging around up there like that. I thought if we made it bump against the brass hard enough it might go off. I would try to make it sway more and he would think my rocking meant heat and tighten his arms around me.

Anyway, none of this has much to do with Christmas, I guess. The whole thing seems like one big drag to me these days and I'd probably just hide out every year until it was over if it wasn't for the kid. I don't think I will try to get him to give me any of those Columbia decorations either, now that I think about it. The Christmas we spent there isn't one I especially want to remember. It was too hot in South America for one thing. Bogata may be like San Francisco at night, but in the daytime, it's just hot, and the air is too thin, and the soldiers are always walking around with their fatigues tucked into their boots. Besides, he made me leave the kid back in the states at my sister's house, so it didn't feel like Christmas worth a damn to me.

This year, I think I'll just go for the old dime store stuff. Red and green balls and a couple of packs of icicles. Maybe the kid can pick out a couple of special things. Knowing her, she'll pick something with Snoopy on it. Or Kermit the Frog, but that's okay. You can't see what's painted on the balls when you're lying under the tree anyway. What you see most are the lights.

The problem is I always want Christmas to be like in that poem by Dylan Thomas where this little kid and his brother wander around all day throwing snowballs with their friends, and singing carols off key. Then they go home and eat turkey and plum pudding and watch their uncles drink too much port wine and nod off after dinner, and their maiden aunts drink too much of the same, and burst into several minutes of frenzied song, and then dissolve into spinster tears. There's always a fire and the best toys and sweets in little bags and somebody strong enough to carry you upstairs and tuck you in at night.

Christmas never feels that way to me, but then Atlanta is a long way from Wales. Full-bosomed aunts in purple knit dresses are a long way from bored Santas in bright red snowsuits and the only people who want to carry me to bed are offering danger, not protection.

But the kid likes to celebrate it, and I guess that's the deal. It's just that this time of year makes me feel a little sorry for myself because it's over. Sorry for myself because it never ends.

Guilty because I am not hungry or cold.

Guilty because I am *so* hungry, and it is *so* cold.

Mixed Drink

(for Kalia)

Her father used to park her
around the corner from the liquor store
so she wouldn't see him going in
and have to lie to her grandmother.

Her mother taught her
how to make Manhattans
and died at home in bed
with a boyfriend who had
no experience in such matters
and greeted the fact of it
by screaming naked in the street
until the police came
and took charge of things.

Now she wants to tell her stories.
She dips her pen
in memories and vermouth
and mixes them well.

Monogamy Blues

I hadn't been to a wedding in a while. The last one I attended was as a favor to a friend and my participation could only be described as a disaster. The confusion began during an after-dinner conversation several weeks before the actual nuptials with me confessing, when pressed by this friend of my friend, that I thought marriage was the death of love. And it ended several weeks after the ceremony when the friend of my friend reviewed the video tape of the ceremony and spotted my face among the assembled well-wishers. "She looked like she thought I was committing suicide," he complained bitterly. "What kind of way is that to look at a wedding?"

From this, I learned two things. First, to keep my eye on the video camera and my expression noncommittal. Second, that I need to stop going to weddings. Period. It's not that I don't enjoy the pageantry. I like to see who's there and peek at who's wearing what and giggle about who was slow dancing with whom in the shadows at the after party. All of that is fine. The problem is the ceremony itself, the monogamy ritual wherein the man and the woman stand before God and the assembled company and promise to forsake all others and cleave only to each other till death do them part. Now it's not that I object to such fine, romantic ideals. It's just that I don't believe them anymore and as far as I can tell, most of the people taking the pledge don't believe them either.

I remember going to a wedding a decade or so ago and being startled when, instead of pledging till death did them part, the couple pledged to remain together only as long as love should last. At the time, I thought such a statement was an admission of defeat before the battle had even gotten started good. Back then, I still wanted to believe that true love was eternal and that

71

the cornerstone of any serious coupling had to be a set of tradi-
tional vows delivered with great solemnity and properly filed
at the appropriate courthouse. The idea that there was another
way to look at things seemed a little bohemian even for my
taste. After all, Atlanta is far enough away from the Left Bank
to make the question of serious revisions in the Moral Code
a moot point.

But that was ten years ago. Since then, I've watched almost
everyone I know divorce. Painfully. I've read statistics that tell
me over fifty percent of all marriages in California now end in
divorce. I've seen the studies that tell me how few people actually
practice monogamy, although almost everybody still promises it
loud and clear when the preacher demands it. I've watched my
married friends drive each other and most of the rest of us crazy
trying to catch each other in lies that wouldn't have been lies if
they hadn't promised the impossible in the first place.

And perhaps most important to my wedding phobia is that I've
developed a feminist consciousness that allows me to understand
the inherently sexist nature of a ceremony in which the let's-all-
pretend-she's-still-a-virgin bride is given by one man to another
as if she were a child or a herd of prize goats.

It was probably a combination of these factors that made my
expression less than felicitous at my friend's friend's wedding.
This probably also caused me recently to break out in a cold sweat
when I pulled up in front of a church with white balloons fluttering
outside to watch two of my own friends take their vows. I don't
know why I went. Perhaps because the groom is an old comrade
from a hundred political campaigns. Perhaps because of the
sweetness in the expression of the bride-to-be. Or maybe because
a part of me was hoping that in the face of all the evidence that
shows the old ceremony is clearly a foundation of sand, my young
friends had come up with a new set of vows based on love and
truth and respect and freedom and equality. Maybe it was because

there is a part of me that wants someone to develop new vows that can sustain us in the face of all that encourages us to lie, to pretend, to box ourselves into forms and rituals and property agreements that have nothing to do with love and trust and everything to do with possession and control.

But that's asking a lot for a warm May evening in a candlelit sanctuary where three ministers held court and the bride wore white and walked delicately up the aisle on the arm of her father to be given in holy matrimony to her properly nervous husband-to-be. Somehow it all seemed like a fairy tale to me—my tuxedo-clad friends and the beautiful bridesmaids and the tiny flower girl with her sash tied just so in the back. I found myself hoping that this time would be different and when the video operator aimed his insistent light in my direction, I crossed my fingers for luck and smiled for the camera.

Mexico Love

Once upon a time, a black woman and her husband, both about 50 or a little older, flew from Detroit to Mexico City where they rented a car and drove off into the mountains. The country was beautiful. The people were pleasant and helpful. The maps were accurate and they were alone together outside the United States for the first time in their natural lives. They turned to each other with anticipation and a shyness they did not really understand. They wanted to pull the car over and make love, but they laughed and drove on.

Just as it started to get dark, their right front tire went flat. They had a spare so that wasn't a real problem. She stood practicing her Spanish while he changed the tire. They were beyond the "can you tell me the way to my hotel" stage. They wanted to be able to talk about how they felt. The Plaza del Such and So was only a backdrop for what they were really looking at, which was each other.

A few miles farther down the road, one of their back tires went flat. It was almost dark now, so they pulled over a good ways off the road to avoid getting hit in the darkness. She was a little nervous, but he didn't seem to be. They were in a tiny mountain village. They will have a phone, he said. We can get another tire and then go on in the morning.

She was relieved. What had frightened her? The darkness? The altitude? The beginnings of the rain?

They found a man willing to fix the tire and a small hotel with huge cathedral windows and a red tiled floor from which a man was sweeping the rain as they approached him in the darkness. Buenas noches, said the man, and my stepfather answered first: Buenas noches. Yes, the man said in patient Spanish after they asked him just as slowly if he had a room for the night, their car had broken down, and they would also like some dinner, if he could recommend a place.

This, said the man, is the place. And he took them up to a beautiful room with a view down the mountain and a painting of the sea and a white bedspread tucked neatly around the huge four-poster bed. My mother stepped out of her shoes and the tile was cool and hard against the bottoms of her feet. She felt beautiful and free. She felt mysterious and sensual. She stood in the window and unbraided her hair.

They had dinner on a tiled patio facing away from the rain. The stark white of the table cloth glowed the way my mother thought the moon might have on a clearer evening. The host said something complimentary of my mother's beauty. She nodded slightly and looked at my stepfather who raised his eyebrows at the man before he smiled back. Gracias.

The man left to get their wine and my mother looked across the table at my stepfather and he smiled at her and took her hand and behind his head she could see the mountains and hear the murmuring of people who spoke a language she could barely understand. She could smell the flowers blooming all around them and the perfume was so sweet she thought she must have put one in her hair and just forgotten. And then she looked into his face and what she saw there was so precious to her, so amazing, so wondrously unexpected that she gasped and felt faint.

My stepfather tightened his grip on her hand. Are you all right? She wanted to say, yes, yes, I'm all right, but she was afraid she might faint before she got the words out. I was so happy, she told me when she told me, that I thought I was going to die. I was so happy....

Their host brought warm ginger ale and when she felt a little better, my stepfather carried her up to their room like he was 25 instead of almost 60 and laid her on the bed and took off her shoes and took the pins out of her hair so he could shake it down around her shoulders and he rubbed her forehead gently and sang to her the way he did at home. And she let out her breath with a sigh, with a rush, that spoke of years of waiting for it, years of hoping for it, years of being afraid it was never going to come around at all, and here it was at last. At last. At last....

Motown Suite

1. Blue Lights In The Basement

FLASHBACK! FLASHBACK! FLASHBACK!
in high school we used to say
"ain't nuthin' but a party!"
which meant nothing short of paradise.
stacks of the latest 45's clicking
into place on the record player,
a blue light for atmosphere
screwed into the socket over the wash tubs,
and when the slow records came on, no lights at all,
or a lock on the basement pantry door
for those who had moved beyond the simple pleasures
of grinding one fully clothed pelvis against another.

"nuthin' but a party!"
and we would dance and drink wine
and hope the thugs did not arrive,
but when they did
(and they always did,
umbrellas that had nothing to do with rain
tapping in front as if they were blind men,
stingy-brim hats cocked in defiance of gravity,
or greasy do-rags wound, rewound
and tied in front, low over the eyes...)
when they did arrive,
we would walk, trancelike, into their arms,
letting them fold their hot, black leather coats

around us,
licking and whispering in our ears,
laughing and growling down deep in their throats,
moaning us into dim corners
until we, choking on our own delighted giggles,
leaned back to look into their eyes,
disapproving and prissy,
pressing our teasing virgin breasts
into their forbidden banlon chests
and wondering what possible sweetness life had to offer
that could be finer than this.

FLASHBACK! FLASHBACK! FLASHBACK!

2. The Ritual Record

It had to be 1959, 1960. I was still a little girl. I don't
remember having breasts yet, but I might have. After awhile,
that kind of thing seems like something that's always been there.
But me and Kris were coming from the beauty shop, so I know
it was Saturday because we only got our hair done on Saturday.
Once a month. In between times, we touched up the edges with
a hot comb that my mother didn't know how to use very well be-
cause her hair didn't need straightening, although ours, coming
to us by way of our father, was still a good ten years away from
coming into style, so we learned to do it ourselves. Well, I
learned to do it. My sister pulled hers back into a big clump,
pierced her ears and became a beatnik, but that's not this story.
    This story is about the record. The Ritual Record. The first
45 record that you buy with your very own money. That first trip

to the record store with your fifty cents clutched in your little hot hand, scared to walk by all the conked head boys hanging around outside the front door, but determined to have the record, and knowing they didn't carry it at Grinnel's downtown, which is where my mother went to buy her Puccini and where you could go into a row of little glass booths and listen to the record before you decided whether or not you wanted to buy it. No, Grinnel's didn't know anything about the music I was looking for.

I was looking for the music that was all black and mostly under 25. I was looking for the music that made you know something g-o-o-o-o-d was coming to you in the next couple of years and even though you weren't sure what exactly it was gonna feel like, you hoped it felt like The Marvellettes and The Supremes and Martha and the Vandellas and Mary "I Got Two Lovers and I Ain't Ashamed" Wells.

You hoped it felt like The Four Tops and Smokey Robinson and Marvin Gaye and The Contours and Junior "I Don't Need No Teeth to Play My Saxophone" Walker. I was looking for Motown. Male Motown. That first time, I didn't want Miss Girl singing about "Baby Love." I wanted the one she was talking to! I wanted to hear the response that was coming from the object of her affections. The ones who made Brenda Holloway feel so bad. The ones who made Tammi Terrell and Kim Weston sound so happy and excited when they were happy and excited. I was looking for Paul Williams and David Ruffin and the rest of the perfectly processed young men who had just released a song called "Dream Come True." I wanted The Temptations.

And I knew where to find them. Up on Twelfth Street or Linwood or Dexter up near the Avalon Theater. All the places my mother was getting increasingly nervous about us going to by ourselves since my sister already had breasts. I do remember that. And she was taller and walked with a long-legged stride front of the record store smile at her and say, "Hey, Little Red!" as she loped on by.

I didn't care. The danger seemed a small price to pay for the pleasures of "Dream Come True." Because when they said that stuff about "I don't care where you came from/I don't care where you been/All I know is that I love you/and I'm gonna love you 'til the end," I wanted to believe it. No. I was only ten. Maybe eleven. I did believe it. Even I was young once. And in love...

3. Remembering Marvin

Well, I guess I was where I should have been when I heard about Marvin Gaye–in the bed. It was Sunday, April Fool's Day and I thought I'd stay out of harm's way. So there I was, sort of half listening to Charles Kuralt on the CBS Morning News when sandwiched in between the Democratic in-fighting and the latest madness in El Salvador, he said that Marvin Gaye had been shot to death in Los Angeles. No details.

No details? Maybe not at CBS News, but my mind is full of details about Marvin Gaye. The kind of details that come at random when all of a sudden he's gone for good. I wanna talk about the details. Not the ones from the end, but from the beginning.

I want to talk about the old days when he used to have enough waves in his perfect process to make you sea sick. I wanna talk about how I believed every word he ever sang to Tammi Terrell and a sizeable percentage of what he had to say to Kim Weston and Mary Wells. I wanna talk about how even though I never could get my mother to understand my obsession with David Ruffin, she always knew what it was I saw in Marvin Gaye. I wanna talk about visiting day at the boy's dorm at Howard University when you had to keep the door cracked open and both feet on the floor, but if your date had sense enough to play Marvin Gaye, you'd probably decide a kiss or two wasn't out of the question.

I wanna talk about a guy who got on the bus once when I was growing up in Detroit with one of those little battery powered record players that folks used to carry when they needed music with them on the street and there weren't any Walkmen yet. How the guy got on the bus with a handful of forty-fives with his name written on the labels of each and every one right under the title of the song, sat down, put on "Stubborn Kind of Fella" and turned it up loud! And the bus driver pulled over and stopped the bus and said, "You gotta turn that down or get off," and the guy stood up without a minute's hesitation and said, "Well, I'll get off then!" And all of us who stayed on the bus laughed and applauded and listened to Marvin's voice going on up the street, singing like a dream.

I wanna say that I tried to resist the message songs at first because I only wanted him to talk straight from his heart to my heart about love, but then I took the time to hear "What's Goin' On?" and I knew it didn't matter what he was talking about as long as it was Mrs. Gaye's son Marvin talking. I wanna say that the sensuality of "Sexual Healing" always seemed to me the logical extension of the absolute romanticism of "Forever" and that I always liked both.

I thought at first the shooting might have something to do with a woman, being old enough to remember Sam Cooke and all. I hoped it wasn't about drugs. I never thought it would be what it was. I don't know how to talk about that part. My friend Zeke says that the hard thing about when one member of the family kills another is that the one you wanna punish is also the one you gotta protect. My daughter says it doesn't seem like he's really dead since his voice is still singing on the radio all the time. Smokey Robinson said that Marvin Gaye was a good friend and would be missed.

81

In "Try It Baby" there's a line that says "Try it baby/you'll see/that nobody loves you like me." Probably nobody ever will love us like that again and sing about it just that way.

Good bye, Marvin. We're gonna miss you. Forever.

Summer Is Coming

the laughter in the street gets louder.
summer is coming
and my brothers clap their hands
and slap their hands
in front of the pool room/cool room/fool room.
summer is coming,
hours filled
with sideways walking
and dreams of naked, perfect women.
the laughter is a constant shout.
heads thrown back
and teeth grinning
in startled white evenness
from the face that always watches...
but summer is coming!
hot enough to make you shine
hot enough to heat the wine,
down inside that plain brown bag,
passing like a hoodoo charm
from hand to hand to hand.
summer is coming,
and my brothers whistle
and sway and say, "hey, baybee!"
as we pass by, pretending
we don't see them on this very same corner
at this very same time
every single day, but hey,
summer is coming,
and my brothers
clap their hands.

Studying The Sixties

My daughter's class is studying the sixties and she asks me for a picture and a memory. What can I tell her? The images that come crowding in are so precious and intense I am afraid to approach them for fear of setting off a self-induced rant that will probably confuse her more than anything else.

Several years ago, a naive question from a creative writing student pushed the same button and when I finally caught myself ten raving minutes later, my students were looking at me with the unmistakable glaze of people whose collective mind has just gone walkabout. I was embarrassed at my inappropriately passionate speech and murmured an apology. Oh that's okay, said a smiling sophomore in the tone people use for small children who can't get across the street unaided. All our sixties teachers go off like that.

I didn't know whether to laugh or cry. I was proud of my generation for maintaining a well-deserved reputation for passionate oratory, but my pride was almost overwhelmed by my sorrow for a generation that has no cause, no commitment, no heroines and heroes to inspire them to throw caution to the wind and take a stand on something.

I was just turning twelve in 1960, which put me right at seventeen when I packed up my great-grandmother's leaving-Montgomery-for-good-and-going-north-at-last steamer trunk and headed down as south as I'd ever been, to Washington, D.C. I was on my way to Howard University as a freshman playwriting major with straightened-to-the-bone bangs down to my eyebrows and a record collection that leaned heavily on Motown, but also included Joan Baez, Bob Dylan, Buffy St. Marie and The Beatles. I had five shades of eye shadow, twenty or so pairs of cheap earrings and two pairs of good ones. I had a panty girdle and tan silk stockings and stick-out bras and blouses with Peter Pan collars that I wore with circle pins at the neckline. I had a copy of The Prophet and a tape recorder to use to send messages home to my father and in my heart I carried fantasies of Greenwich Village and an intensely serious crush on Stokely Carmichael that made me send my food money to SNCC before the first month was half over. I was away from my parents' watchful eyes for the first time in my life, my virginity was intact, and the possibilities seemed endless.

And they were. The sixties were happening like mad all over Washington. Radical poets with bushy beards and burning eyes. Bus loads of our friends arriving from Detroit regularly to march on the Pentagon or picket the White House or lobby our congressmen. Demonstrations on campus demanded black studies, or an end to the war in Vietnam or later curfews, and took place with exhausting regularity. It was and I–we–were all part of it. We read and talked and listened and fussed and cussed and broke out windows and burned down buildings and took it real personal when our eighteen year old friends started getting sent home in body bags two months after the prom. And we played loud music and wore denim bell bottoms and New Breed dashikis and learned to smoke dope and stopped straightening our hair and took off our bras and pierced our ears and my sister even took the bus to Berkeley in search of a sector where our generation was in full control, but it was just a bunch of stoned white kids playing guitar music in the park so she came back home and became a bohemian instead. And Sly got married and they killed or captured all the leaders we admired even a little bit and I stood up in that meeting in tears and said in all seriousness that I couldn't believe how we were talking to each other and couldn't we hear that we sounded just like white people and everybody was ashamed of themselves for such a breach of revolutionary etiquette and tried to do better.

The problem in all this should be obvious. How do I find enough of a way into it to talk about it calmly as a unit of study fit for a seventh-grade class whose hormones are raging and to whom the wonderful energy of 1966 is as remote as the debilitating fear of the Great Depression that had made such a mark on my parents. I don't want it to be history yet. I'm not ready to sanitize and memorize and take a test on what year the assassinations began in earnest, or how many babies were born at Woodstock. It makes it too neat, too organized and safe when the real beauty of it was the wildness. The absolute conviction that we had the right to make the choices each and every minute of each and every day. And we did.

I didn't mean to start ranting and raving, but there it is. I can almost hear my students chuckling sympathetically. Don't worry, they murmur gently. All our sixties teachers talk like that. Well, so be it. Then let the sixties teachers say amen for those days of heaven, throw away the course outline and rant at will. We're beautiful when we're angry.

Cowboys

When my friend asked me to go to an all-black rodeo, I was surprised. My friend is from Texas. Black rodeos are as real to him as Motown is to me, but such activity has no basis in any reality I've ever known. There were no cowboys living on Detroit's west side. How could there be? There were no horses and no space to ride them if there had been any. The men in my neighborhood were exhausted auto workers and grimly resigned postal employees. To me, cowboys were TV fantasy in the way of Robin Hood and Maid Marian. Charming, consistent and absolutely unbelievable.

Cowboys were lean, laconic men who never called women anything but "ma'am" and rarely spoke to each other at all, communicating instead through an impressively varied repertoire of steely-eyed glances. They rode hard, worked hard, handled guns and called Native Americans "red skins" when they got riled. Tall, tight-lipped loners, they were the popular culture's clearest distillation of a seminal white American male fantasy.

Which is the whole point. They were white men. Not occasionally. Not most of the time. Always. From Cheyenne to Sugarfoot, cowboys were big, strong white guys. Now as a child, this wasn't of major concern to me. I simply learned to do what black folks always learn to do, which is to forget about being black for a minute so I could identify with the main character who is always the white character.

We do this consistently. At the movies. Watching television. Voting in presidential elections when Jesse isn't running. It's complicated at first, but the culture is equal to the complexity of the task and we persevere until we train ourselves to be invisible, which is, of course, easier said than done. The process by which a black female child fuses her small ego with that of a six-foot blond white man who is shooting at "Indians" to protect the settlers is convoluted to the point of being totally inexplicable, although not mysterious. Not to black people anyway. How could it be? It is as necessary to our sanity and survival as food and water. Without this ability, how could we go to the movies, buy huge color TV sets and read the daily papers?

It's a fine line, however, even in the most skilled among us. One never knows when race will come rushing in to remind us that we are not The Hero. Ditto The Heroine. It's like when you go to see a Woodie Allen movie and the only black person in the whole thing is the maid, and she doesn't even have any lines. Whether or not this is an accurate reflection of Woodie's world, it hurts your feelings.

But rather than get mad, or go mad, we learn to compromise. To forgive and forget. To identify with Mia Farrow any damn way, no matter how often the invisible maid glides through, silently offering shrimp puffs and champagne. After awhile, it becomes second nature to us. When I went to see "My Fair Lady," for example, I was going to be Audrey Hepburn in that pink silk dress with the high collar if they put Hattie McDaniel, Louise Beavers and Butterfly McQueen all on the screen in uniform at the same time, race pride notwithstanding. And it didn't even feel weird. The idea that the romantic heroine could be a black woman didn't occur to me. There was nothing in the culture to suggest it, and I was, after all, only fifteen. Such an idea was as alien to me as an arena full of black cowboys.

But there they were. Riding and roping and whooping and hollering and looking like The Temptations on horseback. (I think the David Ruffin one even had on chaps!) The problem is how can I tell you what it meant to me to see my first black cowboy at age 37? How can I show you how good it felt not to have to concentrate on not thinking about being black in order to identify with the hero? How can I describe the black kids around me slapping high fives as a giant black cowboy rode a bucking bull for the required eight seconds then swaggered off across the sawdust, as pure an embodiment of absolute macho as I've ever seen? How to determine if I'm betraying a confidence to write about the pride on the faces of the black husbands, fathers, friends watching their brothers make everybody from Buffalo Bill to Clint Eastwood pale by comparison? Where's the language for how fine and mannish they were, effortlessly declaring all attempts at enforcing invisibility null and void?

There isn't any. Just like there isn't any way to really talk about how it feels to see The Dance Theater of Harlem for the first time and realize that ballerinas can have breasts and behinds, or Calvin Peete winning the Masters, or Yannick Noah playing tennis with a headful of dreadlocks.

It was dusk by the time we left the arena and most of the rodeo people were busy outside securing animals in trailers, smoking cigarettes, packing up. At the rear of the parking lot, a tall cowboy was giving children rides on his horse. As he lead the huge, slow-walking animal beside us, my friend suggested that I might like to ride, an offer I quickly declined, awed but not emboldened by the nearness of a real black cowboy. Hearing my friend's coaxing, the cowboy in question tipped his hat at my blushing refusal and grinned. "All pretty ladies ride free, ma'am," he said. No kidding! He actually called me "ma'am." Just like in the movies.

89

The Albino Wino Dreams

stretched into the first
spring sun like a big pink-eyed cat
the albino wino dreams
of twelve month summers
and liquor stores open
around the clock.
the rush hour freeway humming near his head
could be the ocean at high tide
and he smiles in the stupor
which is how he lives
which is what he feels
more than anything lately.
"hey, Red!"
(the others call him Red...)
"hey, Red, you 'wake, man?"
and he murmurs a response
hoping they'll be quiet
and leave him to his dreaming.
what difference can their words make?
he smiles again and stretches
shifting in the sunshine
and in the asphalt wind of urban tides
at hot high noon
the albino wino dreams.

One For The Brothers

Brother Carlton. Brother James. Brother Harold 4X. They are selling *Muhammad Speaks* and talking about the Honorable Elijah Muhammad, disciple of the former silk salesman from Detroit and current self-appointed savior of The Race.

Brother Carlton. Short, big shoulders, broad flat face and a hustler's roll in his walk. Brother Carlton sold suits and shirts from the trunk of his aging black Buick. "Outlet stuff," he would say, explaining that he bought low and sold high, with all profits going toward furthering the work of The Honorable Elijah M.

Brother James was younger and sweeter. He was willing and able to talk about other things while you fished around in the bottom of your purse looking for a quarter. Usually things he had seen on television or heard on the radio. Sometimes local politics and once, just once, his admiration for the quality of love between Romeo and Juliet. Brother James didn't sell clothing. "What would I look like opening my trunk to show a lady a pair of nice pants," he'd say and shake his head. No way. Brother James sold bean pies. A perfect combination of nutritional value and political correctness. All profits going, of course, to the work of the Honorable you-know-who.

Brother Harold 4X didn't sell anything but the paper and he gave away more of those than he sold. Mostly he talked, all day and as far into the night as there might be anybody on the street with a quarter or five minutes to listen. Brother Harold had an older brother who was a famous artist. Avant garde. So famous and so avant garde that he had murals hanging in museums. The murals were horoscopes of fire and blood and winged pigs with pith helmets. Brother Harold's suits were tight and shiny black and day or night he wore green sunglasses and a smile that was saved from being reptilian only by its absolute conviction.

The three had staked out Hunter Street as their territory when I first got to Atlanta at the hot end of summer, 1969. Paschal's Motor Hotel was the center of the strip and one of them was always outside, waving the paper and rapping.

"Sister Pearl," they would say, and if it was Brother Carlton, he might say, "You're looking lovely today, Sister Pearl." Brother James wouldn't say anything. He'd nod and grin and shake his head at Carlton.

I don't know why hearing about Marvin's death made me think of the brothers Carlton, James and Harold 4X. Maybe because I knew them during that time when I called most of the black men I knew "Brother" and had gotten as used to responding to "Habari Gani, Sister!" as I was to hearing "What's happenin', Red?" Maybe it was because Marvin's awesome determination to self-destruct was such an insistent, contrapuntal whine to the brothers' equally awesome determination to survive.

They were all about the same age, give or take a couple of years. Marvin just looked about fifty years older. Teeth rotted or knocked out. Vomit stains crusted on his jacket. Pee on the front of his usually half-opened pants.

Marvin stank, and staggered and spit when he talked. He lurched up and down Hunter Street more regularly than the buses, drunk and begging money with which to get drunker. He terrified the timid among us and disgusted those brave enough to snarl at him when he began his halting, grinning approach, scratching at his matted hair and licking his dry, cracked lips.

He never altered his route and was absent only when he was picked up by the police and taken to jail to dry out. He never did. His first day out, he'd be right back on the street; wild-eyed, trembling and very thirsty. The Brothers had very little to do with Marvin. They knew he was too far gone to recruit, and his presence seemed to distract and depress them. They tended to ignore the hard-core hopeless and focused their attention instead on those who seemed to have at least a little fight left.

But there were stories on Marvin. Most of them centered on the black middle-class respectability of his upbringing. The hardworking sobriety of his parents. Father owned a real estate business, the story went. Marvin, the college-educated son, was to take over the helm and continue on as the flesh of the black entrepreneurial dream.

But Marvin had passion's flame beneath his carefully neutered exterior and he fell in love with a wild woman who drove him mad with desire and doubt, and then left him without a word and disappeared completely. In some stories, there are children involved. In some versions, she doesn't move out of town, merely across it. In one, she kicks him out and maintains the house herself. But in all versions, Marvin is desperate with longing for this woman. He hides outside her house, yearning for a passing glimpse of her. He entreats her by letter and telephone. He thinks of her every waking hour and dreams of her in his sleep.

The details of Marvin's misery are limited only by the imagination of the storyteller, but whatever the improvisational riffs in between, the story always ends with the simple fact that because of this woman–this wild woman–Marvin began to drink and never stopped.

The romance of such a story appealed to me and I found myself eyeing him with a little less repulsion and something like curiosity mixed with awe. Marvin was dying of a broken heart. It was not a common ailment in Atlanta during the summer of 1969 and it seemed more like Heathcliff than Hunter Street, but there it was, happening before my very eyes.

It may have been the romantic extreme of Marvin's life that joined him in my mind to The Brothers. The Brothers also being romantics, embarking as they were on a holy quest for their own fragile manhood. The Brothers—bow-tied knights in shark skin armor, refusing to bend knee to any gods, to any heroes, to any kings, except their own—were as romantic in their way as the passion-crazed lover, howling and moaning and vomiting in the alley behind Paschal's Motor Hotel.

When I finally heard about Marvin's body being found in an abandoned building, I already knew Brother Carlton was out of The Nation. Brother James was selling suits downtown and sporting a mustache and Brother Harold 4X had died in a car accident outside of New Orleans. I had seen Marvin for the first time in years only a few months before his death and was struck by how little he had changed. No better, but not really much worse. I remember being surprised that he was still alive. The story on the street had a final coda on Marvin, explaining the details of his death. It was very simple, really. His father had passed away and left him some houses on Northside Drive. Marvin drank them up in a couple of months and then died of it.

But so did The Brothers. In their own neat, fade-out way. They stepped forward and said, "No!" and then almost died of it. Almost...but they didn't. They just learned how to step back a few paces and regroup when things got too dangerous. Marvin gave up early on regrouping, and then just gave up altogether. It doesn't really matter, I guess. Almost nobody calls me "Sister Pearl" anymore, and the last time I called somebody "Brother" I felt like a fool. The thing is, I thought Marvin's death deserved better than a non-existent obituary and a wino's grave. If the Egyptians were right in claiming that speaking the name of the dead gives some sort of balm to the spirit, then I will speak Marvin's name this one last time in a public place.

94

In the name of romantic obsession, true gallantry, and The Brothers of '69, wherever they might be, may he rest in peace.

Poor Little Hugh

We learned how to ice skate from my Uncle Hugh, invariably called Poor Little Hugh by my grandmother because he was the youngest of three wild boys born to her after she was warned by her doctor not to have any more children because the birth of her first one almost killed her. In addition to the boys, she also had three girls, who could have been called Poor Little Barbara, Poor Little Gladys and the baby, Poor Little Anna Cecelia, also known as Pee Wee, if being younger siblings to their older brothers was going to be used consistently as justification for sympathetic cluckings of the tongue and informed rollings of the eyes.

My Uncle Hugh is also The Quiet Cleage, since by birth we are an opinionated bunch never at a loss for words or convictions. Everyone is passionate about everything. Occasionally, personal lives are examined, but much less frequently than politics. Cleages are not known for their willingness to open up and let it all hang out. I am probably the only one of my generation who indulges shamelessly in public displays of affection, but that could be attributable to the fact that I left home travelling at a rapid clip at age seventeen and have since gone back for only brief intervals in self-defense.

I took the option of removing myself. Hugh took the option of silence. Not hostile silence. Not signifying silence. Just a constant quietness. He heard everything, reacted to it with a rich variety of laughters ranging from slightly amused chuckling to knee slapping guffaws, often followed by coughing, the lighting of another unfiltered Pall Mall, or a bemused shake of the head and an attentively cocked eyebrow.

He was always listening. But talking? Rarely. It was a quality that endeared him to outsiders who saw in Hugh a desperately longed for spark of normalcy which visitors often needed during their first meal with the Cleages. Hugh's completely comfortable silence reassured them in some way that this strange group of eating, arguing, smoking, coughing black folks was not dangerously crazy. Just loud.

Even his brothers and sisters seemed to find relief in the fact that at least one among their number could sit still for a moment without hollering about the state of the race and the assorted vagaries of being black in America. And after he spent twenty uncomplaining years caring for my ailing grandmother, his siblings even began to refer to him as a saint.

But sainthood came later in life. In his younger days, he was the one who went down to the draftboard during World War II and said: "I'm here to enlist. Please give me a rifle and send me South so I can kill every peckerwood I see." Something in the way he said it must have impressed the officer in charge, who gave my uncle the necessary forms and told him to go on home. They'd call him if they needed him.

Much later, someone told me that Hugh walked out the door of the place and didn't remember another thing until he came out of it five miles later, walking across the Belle Isle bridge, laughing out loud so hard he thought his heart was going to burst right there in the shadow of the Miller Brewery. But it didn't.

Hugh learned how to ice skate in Junior High School. He and my Aunt Gladys used to compete in and win all the city-wide meets, and they were good. They wore racing skates, the kind with the blade that sticks out about five inches in the front of the show. These skates are for serious skaters. They don't come in virginal white with little pink puff balls at the ankle. They only come in black. So when he got ready to teach us to skate, Hugh took us out to buy some racing skates and then he showed us how to do it.

How to keep our ankles from bending in—a fate guaranteed to earn you the scorn of the more experienced skaters who leaned effortlessly into the turns of the pond just like the roller skaters at the Arcadia did when anything by Junior Walker and the All Stars would come on. He showed us how to cross over on the turns. How to skate backwards and stop on a dime. And we got good at it. We would go out on Saturday morning and stay until we were so cold everything on us ached and our cheeks were raw and our noses had run and frozen and were disgusting and our hands were too stiff to untie our laces so we'd clump out where weeks of snow had hard-iced over between the tire ridges and skate home in the street.

One Christmas night, we were all sitting around admiring my young cousin's first pair of ice skates and one of us had the brilliant idea that this would be the perfect time to break them in. It was already dark outside, way below freezing, and the river was reputed to be frozen clear across to Canada.

The other grown-ups said it was okay if Hugh would take us so we wouldn't be skating around the Detroit River by ourselves at night while some other non-skating uncle huddled in the car trying to read the latest issue of *The Michigan Chronicle* by the overhead light, getting colder and eviller by the minute. Hugh said okay and went upstairs to get his skates and his earmuffs.

When we got there, it was a lot colder than I thought it was going to be. I had on long underwear, wool tights, two pairs of socks, an undershirt, a tee shirt, a turtle neck, an oversweater, a jacket with a hood and new red mittens. I also had two biscuit, turkey and dressing sandwiches with light mayo and plenty of salt in my coat pockets, but that wasn't so much for warmth as for sustenance, so it is neither here nor there to this story.

When I finally got my skates laced up, Hugh was already stroking up and down the river's edge with his hands behind his back like a sepia toned Hans Brinker and I could hear the blades of his skates cutting through the ice straight and regular as a clock: swish/swish/swish. I skated out to where he was and we skated together for a while. We didn't say anything. He never said anything and I didn't want to open my mouth wide enough to let the Detroit cold hit my teeth. I was happy that it was Christmas night and all that, but I hadn't totally lost my mind.

In the darkness, we could see people skating way out across the river and back. I saw Hugh looking across too, over toward Canada and I knew instantly that he was going to do it. He looked around at me and I opened my mouth long enough to grin back at him and he threw up a hand like he was starting the race himself and cut out toward the other side. I could still hear his skates, faster now but just as even. Swish/swish/ swish. And then it was too dark to see him anymore so I just kept looking in the direction he had gone.

I wondered what he'd do when he got there. Touch it like the base in tag? Plant a flag for god and country? Sing a warrior's chant in honor of the ancestors? Stake a claim and holler free at last?

My Uncle Winslow by marriage is Canadian and when pressed to the wall by a united front of his wife's four implacable brothers, will imply that my family didn't need to be so high and mighty, for if we had been serious about freedom, we wouldn't have stopped at the Detroit River after running all the way from Alabama just because it was November cold and ice flows fast. Even if things were strange enough without changing countries again. Even if this time it would have been by choice.

When I was a kid, I used to think about what it would have been like to run all the way from Alabama to Detroit in the wintertime with no shoes on. I wondered what it would be like to have dogs chasing you. Awful, my mother said. Only savages would send bloodhounds after mothers searching for their children, husbands longing for their wives. Savages. Don't ever forget we were building libraries in Africa while Europeans were still swinging from the treetops. Savages.

When I heard his skates again a few minutes later, he was still stroking in the same rhythm as when he set out. Swish/swish/swish. And then I knew that my Uncle Winslow was wrong. It wasn't that we couldn't get to Canada. We didn't chose to. We had some stuff to finish up here. Some family business to settle. Because if we don't do it, who's going to say all the ancestor's names in public and pour libations on the ground in their honor and set a place at the table for Malcolm X and Samora Machel and Ralph Featherstone and Jimi Hendrix and Zora Neale Hurston and Chester Himes and Langston Hughes and Josephine Baker and John O. Killens and Fannie Lou Hamer and James Baldwin and Nella Larsen and the others, all the others, gone, all gone, but not forgotten.

Pearl Cleage

Pearl Cleage is a prolific writer who works in a variety of formats. She is the editor of *Catalyst* magazine and artistic director of Just Us Theater Company. Her plays include *puppetplay, Good News, Porch Songs, Banana Bread, Essentials* and *Hospice*. First presented by Woodie King, Jr. as part of the Women's Series at the Henry Street Settlement's New Federal Theater, *Hospice* won five AUDELCO awards for Outstanding Off-Broadway Achievement in 1983. *puppetplay*, which premiered at Just Us Theater in 1981, opened the seventh season of the Negro Ensemble Company. Ms. Cleage's performance collaborations include *A Little Practice* (Just Us Theater), *My Father Has A Son* (Nexus Contemporary Arts Center's Club Zebra) and *Love and Trouble* (Seven Stages Theatre). She has also published collections of short fiction *(One for the Brothers*, 1983), and poetry *(We Don't Need No Music*, 1971).

Ms. Cleage has received grant support from the National Endowment for the Arts Expansion Arts Program, the Fulton County Arts Program, the Fulton County Arts Council, the City of Atlanta Bureau of Cultural Affairs, the Georgia Council for the Arts and the Coca-Cola Company.

Ms. Cleage's work has appeared in *Essence, Ms., Black Books Bulletin, The Journal of Negro Poetry* and *Negro Digest*.

Ms. Cleage currently resides in Atlanta, Georgia.

ALSO AVAILABLE FROM THIRD WORLD PRESS

Nonfiction

The Destruction Of Black Civilization: Great Issues Of A Race From 4500 B.C. To 2000 A.D.
by Dr. Chancellor Williams
paper $16.95
cloth $29.95

The Isis Papers:
The Keys to the Colors
Dr. Frances Cress Welsing
paper $14.95
cloth $29.95

The Cultural Unity Of Black Africa
by Cheikh Anta Diop $14.95

Home Is A Dirty Street
by Useni Eugene Perkins $9.95

Black Men: Obsolete, Single, Dangerous?
by Haki R. Madhubuti
paper $14.95
cloth $29.95

From Plan To Planet Life Studies: The Need For Afrikan Minds And Institutions
by Haki R. Madhubuti $7.95

Enemies: The Clash Of Races
by Haki R. Madhubuti $12.95

Kwanzaa: A Progressive And Uplifting African-American Holiday
by Institute of Positive Education
Intro. by Haki R. Madhubuti $2.50

Harvesting New Generations: The Positive Development Of Black Youth
by Useni Eugene Perkins $12.95

Confusion By Any Other Name: Essays Exploring the Negative Impact of The Blackman's Guide to Understanding the Blackwoman
Ed. Haki R. Madhubuti $3.95

Explosion Of Chicago Black Street Gangs
by Useni Eugene Perkins $6.95

The Psychopathic Racial Personality And Other Essays
by Dr. Bobby E. Wright $5.95

Black Women, Feminism And Black Liberation: Which Way?
by Vivian V. Gordon $5.95

Black Rituals
by Sterling Plumpp $8.95

The Redemption Of Africa And Black Religion
by St. Clair Drake $6.95

How I Wrote Jubilee
by Margaret Walker $1.50

Fiction, Poetry and Drama

Mostly Womenfolk And A Man Or Two: A Collection
by Mignon Holland Anderson $5.95

The Brass Bed and Other Stories
Pearl Cleage $8.00

To Disembark
by Gwendolyn Brooks $6.95

Earthquakes and Sunrise Missions
By Haki R. Madhubuti $8.95

I've Been A Woman
by Sonia Sanchez $7.95

My One Good Nerve
by Ruby Dee $8.95

Geechies
by Gregory Millard $5.95

Earthquakes And Sunrise Missions
by Haki R. Madhubuti $8.95

Killing Memory: Seeking Ancestors
(Lotus Press)
by Haki R. Madhubuti $8.00

Say That The River Turns:
The Impact Of Gwendolyn Brooks
(Anthology)
Ed.by Haki R. Madhubuti $8.95

Octavia And Other Poems
by Naomi Long Madgett $8.00

A Move Further South
by Ruth Garnett $7.95

Manish
by Alfred Woods $8.00

New Plays for the Black Theatre
(Anthology)
edited by Woodie King, Jr. $14.95

So Far, So Good
Gil Scott-Heron $8.00

Wings Will Not Be Broken
Darryl Holmes $8.00

Children's Books

The Afrocentric Self Discovery and
Inventory Workbook
By Useni Perkins $5.95

The Day They Stole
The Letter J
by Jabari Mahiri $3.95

The Tiger Who Wore
White Gloves
by Gwendolyn Brooks $6.95

A Sound Investment
by Sonia Sanchez $2.95

I Look At Me
by Mari Evans $2.50

The Story of Kwanzaa
by Safisha Madhubuti $5.95

Black Books Bulletin

A limited number of back issues
of this unique journal are available
at $3.00 each:

Vol. 1, Fall '71   Interview with
                   Hoyt W. Fuller

Vol. 1, No. 3   Interview with
                Lerone Bennett, Jr.

Vol. 5, No. 3   Science & Struggle

Vol. 5, No. 4   Blacks & Jews

Vol. 7, No. 3   The South

Order from Third World Press, 7524 S. Cottage Grove Ave. Chicago, IL 60619. Shipping: Add $2.50 for first book and .50 for each additional book. Mastercard/Visa orders may be placed by calling 1(312) 651-0700.